NOAH DRAKE AND
THE RETURN OF
THE DRAGON HUNTERS

A Christian, Fiction Adventure That Teaches Biblical Creation

By

Ben Russell

Cover Art by Jonna Blankenship

Special thanks to Jemma Russell, Karen Russell and 'Aunt' Martha Henderson for proofing this project

ISBN-10: 198129080X
ISBN-13: 978-1981290802

Dedication

I'd like to dedicate this book to the guys that met with me every other week, for several years, for a morning men's meeting and Bible study. Tim Johnson, Dan Stewart and (in the beginning) Dan Westermier: thank you for sharing your lives with me, encouraging me and being my friend. You may not realize it, but this book series probably wouldn't have happened if it weren't for you three.

Free Activity Set

My family and I would like everyone in your family to enjoy the Noah Drake And The Dragon series, so we put together a fun activity set to go with the books!

Download this kit at http://creationtales.com/activity

You'll get word searches, coloring pages, dot-to-dot and maze activities, plus printable dinosaur sheets.

We hope you enjoy them, thank you so much for reading!!!

Table Of Contents

Table Of Contents

Preface

The Book Of Daniel

Now in that place there was a great dragon, which the Babylonians revered. The king said to Daniel, "You cannot deny that this is a living god; so worship him." Daniel said, "I worship the Lord my God, for He is the living God. But give me permission, O king, and I will kill the dragon without sword or club." The king said, "I give you permission." Then Daniel took pitch, fat, and hair, and boiled them together and made cakes, which he fed to the dragon. The dragon ate them, and burst open. Then Daniel said, "See what you have been worshipping!"

Daniel 14:23-27 (NRSVACE)

CHAPTER 1
THE SLAUGHTER HOOK

The evening was late when a peculiar looking man got to the museum. The sun had set and the building was closed, but the man didn't care. He preferred to come at that time. He wanted to break in to steal something. It was something that was very important to him; something he thought was his property anyway.

The man's name was Edwin Slaughter. He was an old man. His own kids, and even grandkids, were already grown. They were all in jail too!

"They changed the front door," said Edwin, speaking to himself as he approached the old museum. "Perhaps somebody does care about this old place. I would have never guessed."

The place was an old hunting museum. It showcased fantastic and ancient trophies from hunters who were forgotten by time. Nobody seemed to care about the place anymore, except Edwin Slaughter and whoever changed the front doors.

On Edwin's last visit the front doors had been commercial glass, the kind you can see everything through. But Edwin kicked them in so he could sneak inside and steal an old Gatling gun called the Dragon Killer. Now the doors were replaced with solid wooden doors.

Edwin placed a hand on one of the doors and pushed. It didn't move. Testing a little further, he rammed his shoulder into the door. "Ow," he hollered. It still didn't budge.

"Solid as a rock," Edwin said to himself. "No matter, there must be a way inside."

He walked around to the right side of the building. There were a number of windows, each one blocked by a set of bars.

"Wow," he said. "They've really stepped up the security! Even if a window were left open I couldn't get through the bars. This place is sealed tighter than Fort Knox!"

Edwin rounded the back of the building and saw a back door for the employees. "Maybe," he said, "someone forgot to lock the back door." He pulled on the handle, but it didn't move. "Nope, it's locked and secure."

There were no openings anywhere and Edwin began to feel desperate. "I can't do this without Dad's hook. I have to get inside."

Rounding the last corner, Edwin noticed a possible opportunity. A large air conditioner was hanging through a closed window. The machine was mounted on a solid, wooden frame. It was up high, but maybe Edwin could somehow loosen the frame and pull the air conditioner out. That would leave the window open so he could get in.

"This may be my only chance," said Edwin.

He stepped up to the air conditioner and jumped to grab it. He hung onto the side, hoping his weight would pull the machine out, but nothing happened.

Next Edwin swung from side to side, trying to throw his weight as much as possible. He hoped the machine would move a little under his weight, but it didn't.

"Even this thing is solid!" said Edwin. "The owner of this place isn't taking any chances!"

Neither was Edwin. He pulled himself up and on top of the machine. Edwin was old so it took some time, but he had the persistence to get on top.

By now, the sky had turned dark and it was getting hard to see. Edwin sat on the side of the machine and kicked at the two-by-four frame that held it. The air conditioner still didn't move. Neither Edwin's weight, nor his kicking, seemed to make a difference.

"Well, I'm out of daylight and I have nothing to lose," he said. "I might as well throw caution to the wind."

He awkwardly stood on top of the air conditioner. There wasn't much room, but he began to jump up and down. His weight came down hard on the machine and after a minute it started to budge.

"I'm getting it!" he said excitedly. "It's starting to move!"

11

Then, without warning, the air conditioner ripped from the window and fell to the ground. Edwin fell with it, landing on top.

"Owwww," Edwin hollered. "Oh, my back!" He slipped off and rolled back and forth on the ground. "I'm getting too old for this stuff, holy cow."

He laid on his side for a few minutes and rubbed his back where he hit the air conditioner. "This is really going to hurt in the morning," he said.

Finally, Edwin remembered the window. He looked up and noticed it was wide open. A smile came to his face. He stood up and looked at the fallen air conditioner.

"You stupid thing, you hurt my back." He kicked it as hard as he could, then hollered in pain. "My foot!," he said. "Ow, my foot!"

Edwin stumbled around for a minute and griped about how dumb the air conditioner was. After he settled down from his tantrum, he propped up the machine below the window. He used it as a foot stool and climbed into the building.

The room, inside, was dimly lit by an old soda machine. There was also a snack machine and a table with four chairs.

"I must be in the break room," he said.

He made his way to the door and stepped into the next room. It was completely dark. Edwin pulled a flashlight from his pocket and flipped it on. Immediately he jumped and dropped the flashlight. A giant snarling gorilla had been standing directly in front of him.

"Oh my gosh," exclaimed Edwin. "I almost forgot this was a hunting museum!"

He stood, picked up the flashlight and shone the light onto the gorilla's face. "I can't imagine hunting you," he said. "You look ferocious."

Shining the light down he noticed the gorilla was holding a clipboard and a pen. Except for the snarling face, it looked like it was ready to take notes, like a secretary. Edwin moved the flashlight down to a plaque beneath and read it out loud.

"This gorilla, named Penny, was once a business partner to the famous T.W. Gerry. Gerry was famous for his ability to talk to, and train, gorillas. Penny was his prize pupil."

"You have to be kidding me," said Edwin. He continued reading, "Penny didn't hunt. Gerry didn't trust her with a gun. Instead, she worked to create a written language for her fellow primates. At least, that's what Gerry claimed. Penny died before a final language could be created. The only proofs of her writing were some pictures of bananas."

"Written language my foot," said Edwin. "T.W. Gerry was bananas!"

He looked into the snarling face and added, "Penny, you scared me half to death, but you won't do that anymore." To prove it, Edwin punched the stuffed gorilla in the stomach. An indentation was left in its belly.

"That's what I think of you and your partner T.W. Gerry," he said.

He shone his flashlight around to explore the room. He now stood inside the African hallway. Stuffed lions and tigers stared into space, a few of them looked like they were attacking the air.

"Perfect, I know right where I'm at," said Edwin. He

turned and walked to the end of the hall.

Inside the next room was a giant creature. It looked almost like a man, except it was covered with thick, brown hair. Its hands were raised high, as if to scare away troublemakers. Edwin stopped and shone his flashlight at the creature. Its sharp teeth were bared in a menacing growl.

"You look nothing like the Bigfoot I've heard about," said Edwin. "Nothing like him. You're too mean." He turned his flashlight and walked into the next room.

An enormous dinosaur-like creature hung from the ceiling. It had fins instead of legs and feet. The dinosaur had a long neck that stretched across the room and ended with a shovel-shaped head.

Edwin stepped up to a wall and shone his light on a display. A picture of a man with a white, grizzly beard stared at him. His eyes were the same as Edwin's. If it weren't for the beard, you might swear the man in the picture was Edwin.

Edwin moved the flashlight down and found what he wanted, a giant hook. The hook was mounted in front of the picture, as if the grizzly looking man was holding it.

"There it is," said Edwin. "The Slaughter Hook!" Edwin shone the flashlight into the face of his father's picture. "I found your old recipe Dad, the recipe for the bait." He looked into the eyes of the man in the picture. "I tried the Gatling gun, the Dragon Killer, but it didn't work. Champ knocked over our boat and the gun sank to the bottom of the lake." The grizzly man's eyes seemed to scold Edwin. "You're right Dad, you're right. I'm sorry, I should have known better."

Edwin looked at the hook. "You caught him with the Slaughter Hook and bait, right? I might as well do the same. Maybe that would be more honorable to you."

Edwin stood there a moment, wishing the picture of his dad could talk. Maybe Edwin was getting tired, but the picture's eyes seemed to soften. Edwin nodded his head and pulled the hook off the display. He began to walk away, but stopped to look back.

"Wish me luck Dad, I'm gonna need it," said Edwin. "If I want to get this done, I'm gonna need all the help I can get! Everyone thinks I'm nuts. There's a few who don't, but they don't want me to catch Champ anyway."

He paused a bit and looked into his father's eyes. "I miss you Dad. I really wish you were here. You and me, off to catch that old dragon."

Edwin smiled and looked at the picture. His dad almost seemed to smile back.

"I love you Dad," he said. "I miss you."

He looked at the picture a moment longer, then turned and sulked away. He made his way through the darkened rooms, punched the gorilla in the stomach one more time, and jumped out the lunch room's window.

On the way out, Edwin landed on the air conditioner that he left on the ground. He'd forgotten it was there. He twisted his ankle when he landed.

"Oww," he yelped. "My foot, again!"

He jumped around for a bit.

"That's going to hurt in the morning," he said.

After a moment he was able to stand on his foot. He

15

stared down at the air conditioner.

"You stupid thing," he said. Then, in a fit of anger, he kicked it.

He screamed, "Oww my foot!" and hopped around some more. After a few more moments, he finally hobbled into the darkness.

Chapter 2
Hunting For Fossils

"I found something, oh I found something!" shouted Noah Drake. He was bent down on the ground brushing dust away at a dinosaur dig site in the state of Utah.

He loved dinosaurs. He could tell you all the dinosaur names and he'd even learned when and where some of their bones had been dug up in America.

Noah was still young, only twelve years old. Most adults wouldn't think a boy his age could know much about dinosaurs, but he did.

Of course he knew all the normal dinosaur related stuff for a boy his age. He'd seen all the Jurassic dinosaur movies.

He even read the books, which he liked better. He had played all of the common dinosaur video games, his favorite was Dino Farm. Being a total dinosaur nerd, he had even found a website listing all of the dinosaur video games that were ever made. The games went back as far as the original Nintendo and Sega Genesis. Noah hadn't yet played them all, but he had been through about 60 so far. He even tried the game with that old purple dinosaur, you know, the one that teaches manners and how to say thank you. Noah thought he might learn something, but he didn't. That game was meant for infants. Maybe, he thought, his brother Nathan would like it better. Really, the game was meant for someone younger, but Nathan had been getting on Noah's nerves over the past year. Noah told himself the purple dinosaur game was perfect for someone of Nathan's intellect.

Noah also collected dinosaur action figures. He liked the ones equipped with laser cannons or grapple hooks the most, they were more fun. But Noah's favorite was the platinum branded, realistic edition Tyrannosaurus rex. He got if for Christmas the previous year. It came as a complete set with a green screen background, for making animated videos online, and even a history book on the T-rex and where it lived. Noah loved it. It was an exact replica of an adult T-rex, only it was one-fifteenth the size. Even so, it was three feet tall. Imagine how big the real thing would be when it's 15 times larger!

Noah loved dinosaurs, but what made him even more different from the average dinosaur-crazed kid was the fact that he had seen a living dinosaur in person! Yes, a real live dinosaur. He had been on vacation with his Uncle Jim last year at Lake Champlain and witnessed Champ, America's Loch Ness Monster. Most people wouldn't believe it though. Noah didn't have any tangible proof. He saw Champ, but people today don't believe first hand accounts. They need more than that.

Even with the first hand sighting, and his love for all things dinosaur, you normally wouldn't find a twelve-year-old boy at a real dinosaur dig in Utah. Noah was very fortunate. He had won a grant through a student competition that paid him to be here. Who says homeschool kids don't learn anything?

Noah had been the youngest child to sign up for the competition, but he blew the rest of the competition away. The contest was supposed to single out the most brilliant students in America today, and then reward the highest winner with a real life dinosaur dig.

Noah thought the contest was simple. He merely did a history report on his favorite subject, dinosaurs. His was different though. Seeing a real live dinosaur gives you a different perspective. Most other students simply quoted dinosaur digs and findings by scientists in their reports.

For example, did you know that there is no such thing as a brontosaur? That was the name scientist O.C. Marsh gave to an incorrectly pieced together dinosaur in the 1800s.

Marsh got the bones during his own dinosaur dig, but he had put the wrong pieces together. He had paired the body of an Apatosaurus with the head of a Camarasaurus. Marsh called it a Brontosaurus, but since the parts were wrong, that dinosaur never existed.

It was too late once the truth was known. The

Brontosaurs name had caught on and most people thought they knew what it was.

That was one of the common things reported by other students in their reports. It's very interesting history, but when fifty students report the same thing, contest judges get a little bored with the subject.

Noah reported on what he knew best. He believed dinosaurs still existed, so he reported on unusual dinosaur findings that scientists didn't normally approve of.

For example, did you know that in 1925 the carcass of a strange sea monster washed up onto Monterey Beach in Santa Cruz, California? Today it's commonly known as the Monster of Monterey or the Sea Monster of Santa Cruz. Pictures of the body are available and its skull is on display at the California Academy of Sciences.

Scientists decided the monster was a form of Baird's beaked whale, though the twenty to thirty-foot neck and the elephant-like legs don't seem to help that theory.

Some people suggested it was a kind of plesiosaur. Scientists disagree, plesiosaurs were supposed to have gone extinct millions of years ago. It's interesting to note that locals had reported sightings of a mysterious long-necked sea monster in that area before. They had a name for it, Bobo.

Still, scientists couldn't believe the thought that the body of a plesiosaur washed up on the beach. It was just impossible. That would mean plesiosaurs were still alive in the 1900's, or that one had been frozen during an ice age and somehow thawed out and floated over to the beach in Santa Cruz. Either idea was too much to believe. They were both considered impossible, and things like that are usually ignored and forgotten. It doesn't matter if there's scientific proof.

Noah's report faced this problem from a dinosaur bone digger's point of view. He thought scientists could use a worldwide way of reporting when the body of a dinosaur or strange creature is found.

"I think," Noah had written, "we should create a standard way to measure things we find, whether it's at a dinosaur dig or a chance finding on Monterey Beach. Sure, we have pictures and even a skull from the monster, but maybe there's a way we could have more information. Maybe we can take pictures of every body part, take video of every bone and piece them together in a project that scientists all over the world will understand. Perhaps we create a wiki-page online so people can study the evidence on their own. After all, if there were a standard for recording evidence, we might have more proof whether the Monster of Monterey was a whale or a plesiosaur."

The contest judges loved Noah's report. In fact, the comments in Noah's review said, "We need more students like you Noah Drake! We want students who see how complex and important the research of dinosaurs can be.' The winning report landed Noah on a two-week dinosaur dig in Utah. Noah was the only homeschool student on the team, but he definitely had the respect of his leaders.

Now that Noah had found something in the dirt at the dig site, his leaders would respect him even more.

"I can't believe I really found something!" shouted Noah. There were a series of bones sticking out of the ground.

Noah used a brush, much like a paintbrush, and wiped the ground away from the bones he had uncovered. "It looks like some toes. Maybe it's a whole foot!"

A lab assistant suddenly appeared by Noah's side. The young man watched Noah brush away the dirt. "I think you're right Noah," he said excitedly. He pulled out a brush of his own and began to help, anticipating the direction Noah was going. "It looks like it could be another Camarasaurus," said the assistant. "We've already found a couple others on this dig."

"Cool!" said Noah, still brushing the dirt away. "I read how scientists believe they flocked across the northern United States."

"Yeah," said the assistant. "And did you know that we found one, an almost complete skeleton, at the Dinosaur National Monument?"

"Awesome," said Noah.

"I know, right?" said the assistant. "It's the most complete Camarasaurus we've found around here."

"Maybe this one will be better," said Noah, grinning. He continued pushing dirt away from the bones.

Doctor Great suddenly appeared behind Noah. He was in charge of the dig. He'd been the one that made the contest for students like Noah to get their trip paid for. Everyone liked Dr. Great. In fact, that was the nickname students had given him. His real name was Doctor Jim Alexander. Students who liked him began to call him Alexander the Great, and then eventually Doctor Great.

Dr. Great bent down behind Noah and peered over his shoulder to see the bones. "Ohhhh, you found a

Camarasaurus!" he said.

"I knew it!" said the assistant. "I knew it was a Camarasaurus!"

"You were right!" said Dr. Great. "You're getting pretty good at this!"

"We were just saying we hope this one will be an entire skeleton," said Noah. "More complete than the one from the Utah National Monument."

"Let's hope so," said Doctor Great. "It won't be long now and we'll find out! I can already tell you one thing, this dinosaur is big. These toes are quite a bit larger than the others we've found. This must have been a full grown adult!"

Chapter 3
Slaughter Escapes

It was almost five o'clock as inmate number 00819, known to the prison guard as Slaughter, was being transferred to a jail in Burlington, Vermont. Slaughter had been held in the New York state pen but he recently requested to transfer to Vermont. He wanted to be closer to family.

Slaughter was known in New York for his natural tendency to do whatever thoughts popped into his head. He was cruel. He didn't care much if you had nice stuff, because stuff didn't appeal to him. But if you had a position of authority and looked like you had an easier life, watch out.

Slaughter was hungry for power.

You might have a nice looking watch but Slaughter wouldn't really care. However if you got that watch because you were important, then Slaughter would take it and put you on the ground in the process. Slaughter could do unthinkable acts of cruelty and he did them quickly. It was always over before the victim knew what had happened.

That's because Slaughter didn't think about it. He never took time to plan things out. He merely acted on his desires when they came up. If an impulse came that said "Punch that guy in the nose" or "Wipe that smirk off his face," Slaughter would do it! Naturally, he had no friends. When in jail, he usually wound up in the deepest, darkest cell.

When he was younger, Slaughter had dreamed of becoming the president of the United States of America. He had high hopes for a bright future, but those dreams were lost as he grew. Slaughter had street smarts and could usually figure out how to get what he wanted, but he was not smart enough for a legitimate job. He eventually decided that if he wanted anything, he had to force his way in and take it. He didn't have brains but he did have brawn. He could usually take whatever he wanted, and he did.

Slaughter came from a growing line of criminals in his family. His father, Floyd Slaughter, had been in jail since the 1980's for killing two men during a bad drug deal. His grandfather, Edwin Slaughter, had always seemed straight, but recently took a bad turn and was wanted for kidnapping and theft. Even Slaughter's younger brother, Frankie, was recently jailed for helping his grandpa with the crimes.

Slaughter, better known to his family as Seth, laughed to

himself. Who would have thought his younger brother Frankie would stoop to a life of crime? Seth would do it in a heartbeat, but Frankie wouldn't. Frankie was too nice. Sure, Frankie would knock you out to steal something, but only because he wanted it, not because he was mean. Seth wondered if Frankie had changed. Perhaps it had something to do with his Grandpa.

What was interesting is that Seth was being transferred to Vermont because of his Grandpa. Gramps told Seth to request the transfer so they could visit more often.

"I've got to see that fool grandson Frankie in Vermont!" Gramps had said. "It'd be nice if I didn't have to drive so far to see you too!"

Seth thought an occasional visit would be nice, so he asked for the transfer. The request went through without question and Seth was moved within the month. The prison guard let him know of the approval and even gave Seth a phone call so he could let his Grandpa know when it would happen.

"Eureka!" Grandpa Edwin had exclaimed. "That will really help! I don't know if I can talk your brother Frankie into doing it, but now you'll be available!"

"What?" Seth had asked. "What are you talking about? Help with what?"

"Don't you mind," said Grandpa Edwin. "You just look for my car. I'll give you a honk and you'll know what to do!"

"Whatever Gramps," Seth had said.

But now that the transfer was happening, Seth remembered everything Grandpa had said. Did Grandpa Edwin have some kind of plan to break him out?

"Nah," Seth said to himself. "No way. He's not that kind of guy."

The prison van slowed and was now approaching the prison in Burlington. They had driven all day and the trip was finally over. Seth looked at the prison as they approached. It was large, but not as big as the one he just came from. He hoped they would have better food here.

The van entered into a large parking lot and rolled over a speed bump. It finally came to a stop just behind an old sports car. Funny, but it looked like Grandpa's old Packard Hawk. They didn't make cars like that anymore. Seth knew, he'd stolen and resold several of them.

The van's driver turned the ignition off, got out and walked to the main gate so he could check in the prisoner. A guard unbuckled from the front passenger seat, opened Seth's door and unlocked his chains to help him get out. Seth stepped onto the pavement and looked up at the prison. It was large and foreboding, but it didn't scare Seth. He was used to being in prison.

The guard pulled on Seth's arm and began to guide him towards the gate. Suddenly a loud honk came from the old sports car. The guard let go of Seth and turned towards the sound, carefully putting his hand on the gun on his side.

The old sports car honked again. Seth realized that it was his grandpa's old Packard Hawk, and Grandpa was waving his hands from the driver's side window.

"Come on you big dummy!" hollered Grandpa Edwin. "Can I spell it out any clearer?"

The prison guard and Seth looked at each other. In an instant they both knew what the other was going to do. The guard began to pull out his gun but Seth beat him to the punch, literally. Seth lowered his fist and gave the guard an uppercut he'd never forget. The guard's body lifted into the air and then fell lifelessly to the ground. He was out for the count and the gun was tossed to his side.

Seth put his hands behind his head and stretched his back. He turned his head to the side and cracked his neck. Things were about to change. Seth was going back into business. He bent down and picked up the gun that the guard had dropped. He pointed it towards the guard and said, "nighty-night mister prison guard."

Gunshots suddenly fired from the prison gate; the guards were attacking. Grandpa Edwin honked his car horn and turned on the engine. Seth's body seemed to act before he knew what to do. He didn't shoot the guard. Instead, his feet were running and he dove into the passenger window of his Grandpa's car. Seth's feet and legs dangled outside the window as the car sped away. He was so large he couldn't manage to get the rest of his body inside.

Before the car was out of sight, an expert marksman from the prison squeezed off a successful shot. The bullet hit Seth's left foot. He hollered in pain and Grandpa Edwin raced the car away.

Chapter 4
Unbelievable Nathan

"Why do creation teachers always talk about a worldwide flood when they want to prove the world was created by God?"

The question was asked by a visitor at Nathan Drake's local creation museum. The man was touring there with his son.

Nathan was volunteering at the museum during the summer weekends. Today he was tagging along with the museum's curator, Professor Will. Nathan got to help guide the tour. He was only ten years old but he already knew a lot about how God could have made the world.

Nathan had to mind his manners to help at the museum. That wasn't hard, he was a very good kid. However, like most boys his age, Nathan had a lot of energy and that energy sometimes got him into trouble. Well, that and his clumsiness.

If you combined Nathan's energy with his natural curiosity, and a need to constantly move around, bad things seemed to happen. It's not that he tried to cause problems, they just seemed to happen when he was around — a lot. If there wasn't some kind of accident or problem, Nathan was probably talking too much and putting his foot in his mouth.

"Seriously," said the visitor. "There are floods all the time. How could one flood make such a big difference to man and creation? Why is it such a big deal?"

"Well," said Prof. Will, "it's because it wasn't just another flood. It was the flood to end all floods. It was a disaster that had never been seen before and it hasn't been equaled since!"

Prof. Will knew a lot about biblical creation. He could often be found leading tours and explaining the credibility of a world created by God. Nathan learned a lot from Prof. Will, and he was always excited to get more information that seemed to make evolution look dumb.

"We teach that it took God six days to create everything we know," said Prof. Will. "That's the whole planet, the land and the sea, plus the stars, the universe and the galaxy. That was all made by one God, with just a few words from his mouth."

The visitor nodded, "Yeah."

"If that's true," said Prof. Will, "if one God could create

everything, don't you think He could destroy it all with one flood?"

"I guess so," said the visitor. "But one flood can't explain everything. I mean, what about all the things that science explains? How could a flood make a difference to how old the dinosaurs are? How could it affect how the continents split and spread out from one giant continent? How does a flood show that creation science is true?"

Prof. Will stepped over to a large display of an ark at the side of the room. The display was intricate showing individual rooms where animals would stay. A stream of buffalo, zebras, giraffes and ducks were climbing a long walkway to go inside.

"You know," said Prof. Will, "if there were just one flood, an all-encompassing world-wide flood, it could destroy everything we know. One flood could move the mountains and carve out valleys. One flood could change the planet as we know it."

"That's right," added Nathan. "It wasn't just a little water rising up. It was a tsunami of epidemic proportions!" Nathan threw up his hands to show how large a flood could be, but he lost his balance and fell into a display of Noah and his wife beside the ark. Noah and his wife fell and almost knocked down the ramp with the animals on the display, but Prof. Will saved it. He knew Nathan and his clumsiness so he had been prepared, just in case something like this happened.

"Yes," said Prof. Will, laughing. "It takes only one Nathan Drake to destroy a Noah's Ark display at the creation museum. It could easily take only one flood to destroy the world when God allowed it!" Nathan giggled while he and Prof. Will picked up the display.

"But, what makes a world-wide flood so terrible?" asked the visitor.

"Can I answer that Prof. Will?" asked Nathan. Nathan had a big conviction to teach about biblical creation. This was partly because he saw a living dinosaur the year before with his older brother Noah.

"Okay, give it a shot," said Prof. Will.

"Thanks," said Nathan. He turned to the visitors and said, "Some Bible teachers believe that it had never rained before the great flood."

"Really?" said the visitor. "I've never heard that before."

"Oh yeah," said Nathan. "Could you imagine how incredible it would be to see rain if it had never rained before?"

"Well, no. I guess not," said the visitor.

"It would be amazing to see water fall from the sky!" said Nathan, stumbling again. "But do you know what's even more amazing?"

"What?" asked the visitor's son.

"If it had never rained before," said Nathan, "why did it start now? Why rain at the time of this flood?"

"Yeah, why?" repeated the other boy.

"It would take something huge to change the Earth's environment like that," said Nathan. "If there had never been rain before, what changed the entire planet to make it rain? And think about it, there's still rain today! The change must have started some new cycle of nature because it's still going today!"

"Well," said the visitor. "What caused it?"

"God," said Nathan. "The Bible says God caused the waters under the earth to break loose. The world split open and water exploded upwards. That new addition of water was enough to change the weather."

"It's possible something else changed too," said Prof. Will. "The Bible says when God created the Earth, He separated the waters below from the waters above. Creation scientists wonder if that means a layer of water surrounded the Earth's atmosphere, kind of like the Ozone layer we have today."

"What's the ozone layer?" asked the visitor's son.

"It's a layer of gas between the sky that we can see and outer-space," said Prof. Will. "It's a chemical that helps protect the planet."

"That's right," said Nathan. "Creation scientists think there could have been a layer of water surrounding the earth, just like the ozone that's there now."

"Wouldn't that just mean that the rain clouds were up there, like they are today?" asked the visitor.

"No," said Prof. Will. "This layer was farther up, where it's so cold that the layer would have turned to ice. You could call it a canopy of crystal that surrounded our planet."

"A layer of ice surrounding the Earth?" asked the visitor. "That's kind of hard to believe."

"I know, right?" said Nathan smiling. "Isn't biblical creation cool?!"

"But," said the visitor, "is there any way to prove there was water above the atmosphere?"

"Maybe this," said Prof. Will. "Scientists can prove that

air used to have more oxygen than it does today."

"Really?" asked the visitor. "How?"

"Because we can find bubbles of air buried with fossils from the past," said Prof. Will.

Nathan interrupted, "They might find it in ancient bits of amber, like that old Jurassic theme park movie. You know, the one where scientists found mosquitoes trapped in amber?"

"That's right," said Prof. Will. "Scientists have found ancient bubbles of air just like that."

"Really?" asked the visitor.

"Yes," said Nathan. "And you know what?"

"What?" asked the visitor.

"That air was different from today's air," said Nathan.

"The chemical structure was different," said Prof. Will. "There was a lot more oxygen! Why would there have been more oxygen in the air thousands of years ago?"

"Yeah, why?" asked the visitor's son.

"I'm glad you asked," said Nathan. He kneeled down beside the boy. "It's because there may have been a crystal canopy of ice surrounding the atmosphere of the Earth. That would explain everything!"

"A canopy of water would make the air we breathe richer in oxygen," said Prof. Will. "Our planet would have been like a huge greenhouse."

"Cool," said the child.

"That is cool," said the father. "Is there any more proof? What else would back up your theory?"

"Well, if the earth had more oxygen in the air we breathe, things that lived here could have lived much longer," said Nathan.

"They could?" asked the visitor.

"Yes!" exclaimed Nathan.

"You see," said Prof. Will, "science proves that the human body heals much quicker when there is more oxygen in the air. That's why sport teams have hyperbaric chambers."

Nathan turned to the visitor's son and said, "Those are rooms with lots of oxygen in the air. They help athletes heal quickly from sports injuries."

"Cool!" said the little boy.

"That's actually an old technology too," said Prof. Will. "Today some doctors do something called Oxygen Therapy. They give patients a shot with oxygen and ozone for their sore joints."

"So," said Nathan, "things would heal quickly if the air, all over the earth, had much more oxygen."

"Plus things would live longer," said Prof. Will.

"They would?" asked the visitor.

"Yes!" said Nathan, standing up to look at the dad. "The Old Testament in the Bible records that people lived to be hundreds of years old before the flood."

"That's right," said Prof. Will. He pointed to the display of Noah and said, "Noah was about 600 years old when the flood happened. The Bible says he lived another 350 years after that!"

"So Noah lived to be 950 years old?" asked the visitor.

"Yes," said Prof. Will. "Noah's grandpa, Methuselah, lived even longer. He was 969 years old when he died!"

"Okay, but let's pretend that the Bible isn't true," said the visitor. "Is there other evidence showing things could live that long?"

"Well," said Prof. Will. "You could consider the number of years it took for a dinosaur to grow huge."

"Dinosaur?" asked the visitor's child.

"Yes," said Prof. Will, looking at the boy. "Have you ever seen a lizard before?"

"Oh yeah!" said the child. "Outside our house! One lives by the backdoor!"

"I have one outside my house too!" said Prof. Will. "Did you know that lizards continue to grow until they die?"

"They do?" asked the dad.

"Yes," said Prof. Will. "All reptiles continue to grow until the day they die. Lizards, alligators and even crocodiles continue to get bigger as long as they live. If reptiles never stop growing, and they could live for hundreds of years in an oxygen-rich environment, how big do you think they'd get?"

The man looked off into space and answered, "As big as a dinosaur." He seemed in awe of the thought.

"That's right!" said Nathan.

"So dinosaurs could have evolved from lizards?" asked the man.

"No," said Nathan firmly. "There's no evolution here. We're just talking about reptiles that live a long time. They can grow quite large because they live so many years."

"Wow," said the man. "That's an interesting thought."

"So what happened to the dinosaurs?" asked the little boy. "Did the flood kill them all?"

"Oh no," said Nathan. "Noah probably took some of them on the Ark!"

"That's right," said Prof. Will. "He probably had a bunch of different kinds. Sure, most were killed in the flood, but there were some that survived with God's protection!"

"Wait a minute," said the man. "How could a huge dinosaur fit on an ark? And wouldn't that be dangerous to have a man-eating T-rex on board?"

"Well Noah was a smart man," said Prof. Will. "He probably took baby dinosaurs. They would be much smaller and easier to work with."

"It'd be easier to pack supplies for babies," said Nathan. "They wouldn't eat so much. Plus, they'd be safer to keep!"

"Then where did the dinosaurs go?" asked the visitor. "Why did they all die off?"

"They didn't," said Nathan. "There's still a few around today! I saw three last year at Lake Champlain!"

The visitor took a step back from Nathan, pulling his son with him. He looked like he had just been slapped in the face. "You saw a dinosaur, last year, in Lake Champlain?"

"No," said Nathan smiling, "I saw three dinosaurs!"

Something seemed to change. It was as if a glass wall was instantly built around the visitors. They stopped asking questions and no longer seemed interested in the museum. It was very awkward. Nathan didn't realize it, but all his credibility was lost with that one comment. The trust the visitors had in the museum was now gone.

The tour continued, but the visitors no longer asked questions. Nathan and Prof. Will tried to tell them about biblical creation, but the visitors just nodded and said "Uh-huh." It made the rest of the tour go quickly.

At the end they both said thanks and hurried out the

door.

CHAPTER 5
JAIL BREAK?

Frankie Slaughter lay snoozing in his jail cell. He hated being here, but he'd grown used to living in prison. It wasn't fair, but he was here because he'd done some bad things the previous summer. He'd helped his grandpa Edwin Slaughter in what turned out to be a complete escapade, and not a good one.

Before that summer's antics, Frankie had tried to stay out of trouble. He had been in jail before and decided any amount of time there was unbearable, even it was only three days. Now he was locked up for three years! At least, that's what they said when he was put in jail.

The misadventure with Grandpa Edwin was about restoring honor to Frankie's great grandfather, Sammy Slaughter. It wasn't a big deal to Frankie. Great Grandpa Sammy had been dead all of his life, but the honor was a big deal to Frankie's Grandpa Edwin.

Apparently, many years ago, Great Grandpa Sammy had caught and killed Champ, the sea-monster of Lake Champlain. It was a big deal and Sammy was supposed to get a lot of money for the monster's body, but something went wrong. Somehow the dinosaur's remains were confiscated from Great Grandpa. The sale never happened and Sea-Monster-Sammy grew infamous for believing he caught something that most people thought never existed. You could say he became the town kook!

Anyway, last summer Frankie's Grandpa Edwin discovered that a sea-dragon was still alive in lake Champlain, so Edwin decided to restore honor to Sea-Monster-Sammy's name. The plan was to catch and kill Champ. Most people would think that was a ridiculous idea. Frankie thought it was a ridiculous idea, but that was before he ran into Champ while on a boat with his grandpa.

An incredible escapade then happened, but in the end Frankie and Grandpa didn't catch Champ. They'd come close, but it didn't work out. The sea monster flipped their boat and got away. Not that Frankie minded. He didn't really like the idea of killing the dinosaur, especially because it had a couple of babies.

A few bad things happened during the escapade. You could say they were really bad things. Frankie had helped kidnap and hold a family hostage. He'd been caught stealing a boat and was also accused of stealing a historic Gatling gun from an old museum. Frankie did do some of those things, he didn't steal the gun, but he had done the other stuff. His grandpa had talked him into it, all for a few tacos. Frankie loved tacos, especially beefy nacho tacos with the special TNT sauce from Tasty Nacho Tacos. It was heaven, but it wasn't worth three years in jail.

The police had caught Frankie while he was trying to return the boat that he and Grandpa had "borrowed." Now he was paying the price for their crimes.

One good thing happened from all of this though. Frankie found salvation, through Jesus, thanks to a young boy's friendliness and heart for The Lord.

This had all happened the previous summer. Today it was approaching springtime and Frankie had learned to be content with his circumstances. He was getting through his time in jail just fine. He had teamed up with some other prisoners for a group Bible study, studied the Bible on his own during the long days and continued a pen pal relationship with his new friends Noah and Nathan Drake.

Once a week Frankie was even awarded his heart's desire, a delicious meal from Tasty Nacho Taco. The jail had worked it out with the judge because Frankie was returning the stolen boat when he got caught.

Today was Frankie's special day. It was customary for him to eat his special meal and then take a long, happy nap on his bed. The day was moving along as usual. Frankie had already eaten his TNT and was now napping, but things were about to change.

A key turned in Frankie's jail cell. The door slid open

and a prison guard named Joe said, "Time to wake up Frankie. You have a visitor."

Frankie woke up with a snort. He sat up and looked at the guard in confusion.

"I said you have a visitor," said Joe.

"But Joe, I've never had a visitor," said Frankie.

"Well you have one today," said Joe. "Some guy named Champ."

"Champ?" repeated Frankie. "What a weird name. I don't remember anyone named Champ."

"Well," said Joe, "maybe he has confidence issues. Anyway, he's waiting in the visiting room right now. Come on, let's go."

Frankie drowsily stood up and stepped out into the prison hall. It was a two-story tall room with prison cells on both levels. Frankie's cell was on the bottom level. He walked in front of Joe the security guard and looked around. Two or three other prisoners stood looking at him from behind closed bars. He recognized a couple and waved at one of them. "Hey Chris," he hollered. "Two more days till our Bible study!"

Chris hollered back, "Cool! I got something to share too!"

Frankie smiled. He really enjoyed his Bible time with the other guys. Joe the security guard led Frankie to a small visiting room at the end of the hall. It was a place Frankie had never yet been, but it looked promising. There was a soda machine inside.

"Joe, there's a soda machine in there," said Frankie. "Does this mean I get to have a soda?"

"Tell you what," laughed Joe. "If you're good, I'll get you a soda."

"Awesome!" shouted Frankie a little louder than you'd expect. It was almost like he was a five year old excited about something simple. "That means I'll get one, 'cause I'm always good!"

Joe laughed and said, "Well, we'll see."

Frankie stepped into the visitor room, eyeing the soda machine. "Root beer," said Frankie. "I think I'll get a root beer if they decide to treat me."

The room was small and, along with the soda machine, held a few circular tables. A man that Frankie didn't recognize sat behind one and smiled. "I think root beer's a nice choice," he said.

Joe, the prison guard, closed the door to the visitor room and stood outside.

Frankie eyed the man behind the table. He was very peculiar, though somewhat familiar. He wore dark sunglasses and what looked like a fake, shaggy beard. Wait a minute. Was that a wig underneath his ball cap? This man was not what he appeared.

The man must have noticed Frankie's hesitation because he spoke up. "It's okay ya big dummy. Have a seat"

"Gramps?" asked Frankie. "Is that you Gramps?"

"Of course it's me," said Grandpa Edwin. "Now sit down before the prison guard gets too curious."

"Oh now I understand why you called yourself Champ," said Frankie, not yet sitting down. "You really had me wondering! But wait a minute, what are you doing here?" He ducked and lowered his voice to a whisper. "Don't you know that you're a wanted man? They'll put you in jail if they know it's you!"

"That's why I want you to sit," said Grandpa Edwin. "And that's why I'm wearing a disguise."

"It's a horrible disguise Gramps," said Frankie, finally sitting at the table. "I don't know if anyone will buy it."

"Well they did," said Grandpa. "Now shut up for a minute so I can talk to you."

Grandpa Edwin looked Frankie up and down for a minute. "You look different. Are they treating you okay here?"

Frankie smiled for a bit. He was excited to get a visit from somebody, especially someone he knew. But suddenly he remembered that this man was the reason why he was here in jail. If it wouldn't have been for Grandpa Edwin, Frankie might still be enjoying the free air and ability to eat Tasty Nacho Tacos anytime he'd like.

"They're treating me fine," said Frankie, "but why do you want to know? You're the reason why I'm here."

"Oh Frankie," said Grandpa Edwin, "I didn't mean for you to get caught. I thought you'd see the cops when they were sneaking up on us at the lake."

"I did see the cops," said Frankie, "but I didn't see you anywhere. You took off and left me to get blamed for all of your crimes!"

"But don't you see Frankie?" asked Grandpa Edwin. "You didn't do anything wrong! You were just trying to help me get Champ so we could honor your great grandfather Sammy."

"Tell that to the judge," spat Frankie. "They gave me

three years for holding the Drake family up at gunpoint, stealing the row boat and for stealing that stupid Gatling gun."

"Look, I'm sorry Frankie," said Grandpa. "I'm sorry that you're in jail. It didn't go as I planned. It didn't go like I planned at all, but I'm here to change things."

"What?" asked Frankie. "Are you going to turn yourself in?"

"What, are you crazy?" hissed Grandpa Edwin. Then, lowering his head, he whispered, "I'm here to break you out!"

"Break me out?" asked Frankie. "What are you talking about?"

"I've got a deal with a couple of the night-time guards," said Grandpa. "But we have to do it tonight! All you have to do is stay awake and walk out of here at 2:15 in the morning!"

Frankie gave his grandfather a disgusted look. "That's it, huh? Just stay awake and walk out of here?"

"Yes," sighed Grandpa. "It can't be any simpler. The guards will let you walk right out the front door. That's where I'll meet you."

"And then what Grandpa?" asked Frankie. "Are we back on the trail of Champ?"

"Of course!" said Grandpa. "And all the Tasty Nacho Tacos you can eat. But we have a little help this time. I broke your brother out of jail this morning."

This news hit Frankie like a ton of bricks. He stared at his Grandpa open-mouthed. Finally he shook his head for the revelation to sink in and said, "You broke Seth out jail?"

"Yes!" said Grandpa Edwin. "He said you'd be speechless when I gave you the news! Isn't it exciting?"

"No, it's nuts Grandpa!" hollered Frankie.

Joe the security guard knocked on the window. Frankie turned to look at him. Joe held up two fingers and mouthed the words, "Two minutes." Then, looking more carefully at Frankie he mouthed the question, "Is everything okay?"

Frankie nodded yes and turned back to his grandfather. "Listen Grandpa, Seth's a real criminal. He was in jail for trying to punish a couple of other criminals for trying to take over his chop-shop."

"I know Frankie," said Grandpa Edwin. "It'll be all right. He owes me for getting him out."

"Gramps," said Frankie, "it's not going to go well. You watch. The tides will turn and Seth will make your bad idea an even worse idea!"

"That's why I need your help," said Grandpa. "Between you and me, we'll be able to make sure everything goes well."

"Mmm, no," said Frankie. "I'm out."

"What?!" exclaimed Grandpa Edwin. "We're talking about freedom Frankie. It'll be fun, plus all the TNT tacos you can eat..."

Frankie laughed. "Getting stuck in another escapade with you and Seth is not freedom Gramps. That's far from it. I think I'm better off staying here in jail."

Grandpa Edwin took his sunglasses off and looked Frankie straight in the eye. "Better off in jail? What's gotten into you Frankie?"

Frankie looked down at the table and shook his head. Then, looking at his grandfather he said, "Jesus, Jesus got into me Gramps. I'm learning all about Him here in jail."

"Oh Frankie," said Grandpa, ignoring Frankie's testimony. "I so wish you'd help us out."

"You know what Grandpa," said Frankie, "Jesus really helps me out. I think He could help you too. Maybe if you spent some time with me you could learn about Him."

Edwin Slaughter stood up. "What are you saying Frankie? Are you threatening me?"

"No, I'm not threatening you Gramps," said Frankie. "I'm just saying it like it is. You're supposed to be here in jail with me. Maybe some time in here would do you good, give you a chance to fix things in your life." Frankie turned towards the prison guard.

"Wait Frankie," said Grandpa. "Here, take this." He handed Frankie a dollar bill.

"A dollar?" asked Frankie. "What's this for?"

"Root Beer," said Grandpa, putting his sunglasses back on. "I want you to get a root beer."

A big grin filled Frankie's face. "Thanks Gramps," he said. Then he scowled, realizing his grandpa might be trying to pull a fast one. "This doesn't change anything. I'm still gonna tell Joe you're here."

"I know Frankie, I just want to make sure you get a root beer."

"Okay," said Frankie, "thanks!" He took the dollar bill and skipped over to the soda machine. It took his dollar bill and he pushed the root beer button. Nothing happened. He pushed the button again and waited. Still, nothing happened.

"What's going on?" he said to himself. Then he noticed the price on the machine. It clearly said two dollars. "Hey Gramps," he said, "I need another dollar." He looked towards his grandpa, but Edwin was no longer there. He had snuck out while Frankie was distracted.

"It figures," Frankie said to himself. "You left me again. I'm a day late and a dollar short!" Frankie knocked on the window. "Hey Joe, you better come in here. I got something to tell you. Hey, you got an extra dollar?"

CHAPTER 6
FOSSIL DATING

Noah Drake was having the time of his life. He'd been playing in the dirt, digging for dinosaur bones for almost an entire week. Any other child would have been instantly bored, possibly giving up six days ago after the first hour. Not Noah, he loved it! And now he had found some real dinosaur bones! Not limestone, like the "fossils" he found in his own yard. These were real Camarasaur fossils, even identified by Dr. Great!

Ten other students and assistants had now gathered around Noah's Camarasaurus. They were all carefully uncovering the old bones. Each person worked slowly, but with excitement. So far four dinosaur legs and a few ribs had been found.

"I can't wait to tell my family," said Noah. "They're going to be so excited. Well, maybe not my brother Nathan. He'll probably be jealous, but everyone else is going to be excited!"

"You don't think your brother will be excited?" asked Doctor Great.

Noah thought for a second. "Well, he'll probably think it's cool, but I doubt he'd be very happy. He's been too jealous of this whole trip. He really wanted to do it too."

"Oh Noah," said Doctor Great, "give your brother a little slack. I'd have been upset if my brother got to do this and not me. This is exciting stuff! Surely he'll be excited for you."

"Well maybe," said Noah. "But it's not a big deal if he's not."

Doctor Great seemed okay with this response. He didn't add any more to the conversation.

In truth, Noah knew his younger brother did like dinosaurs. In fact Nathan liked them nearly as much as Noah, but dinosaurs were Noah's thing. They had always been his thing. Nathan just copied off of Noah and sometimes followed in his footsteps.

Nathan may have been a copycat, but he and Noah had always been the best of pals. That started to change though, not long after their last family vacation. During the trip Noah and Nathan had an awesome adventure at Lake Champlain. They even got to see Champ, the lake monster that was rumored to live there. The two boys found out

Champ was a giant plesiosaur and even had two babies. It was a glorious time. Noah even helped save Champ from extinction, but things had changed since then. Nathan had changed, perhaps Noah had changed too.

Both boys were growing up. Right now they just didn't get along. They were each like sandpaper, grinding on each other. They were finding their own personalities and forming their own opinions. You could call it sibling rivalry. That's just a fancy way of saying that sometimes brothers and sisters don't get along.

"I think I found the tail!" hollered one of the students helping uncover the bones. The excitement brought Noah back to reality. He had actually discovered something amazing and the Camarasaurus was starting to look like a real animal, not just a pile of bones. It was very cool.

"I wonder how old it is," pondered one of the students.

"Aren't they all about a hundred and fifty million years old?" asked one of the students.

"Give or take fifty million years," answered Noah's assistant. "That's what radio metric reports say. This Camarasaurus lived a long, long time ago."

"I assume you're testing the rocks to find their age and then guessing the dinosaur bones are the same," said Noah.

"Yes," said Dr. Great. "We use a chronometer to test the rock. There is Uranium-lead inside. We measure how much there is to decide the age. This section of rock is about a hundred and fifty-million years old."

"But don't you think they could be younger?" asked Noah.

"That's up for anyone's opinion I suppose," said Dr.

Great. "This dinosaur could be younger. It just depends on how we read the Uranium-lead count. It's the best test there is to find out something's age."

"Could you test to see how much Carbon-14 is in it?" asked Noah.

"Carbon dating? No, that would be a waste of time and money," said Doctor Great.

"Why?" asked one of the students. "What's the difference?"

Doctor Great had been helping clear off the dirt, but now he sat back on his feet. "Well," he said, "they both work the same way. Uranium-lead dating measures how much Uranium-lead is inside something. Carbon dating measures the amount of Carbon-14. Both of those elements are in everything, but over time they rot away. We can guess how old something is based on how much Uranium-lead or Carbon-14 is still inside. Noah, Carbon-14 only lasts fifty-thousand years. It's all gone after that. This dinosaur's bones are millions of years old. We can't carbon date it because there won't be any C-14 inside, it's all gone by now."

"But what if there is Carbon-14 inside?" asked Noah. "What if this dinosaur is younger than fifty-thousand years?"

"Don't be silly Noah," said one of the students.

"Yeah," said another. "Dr. Great said we already know the rocks are millions of years old."

"But what if the Uranium-test is wrong?" asked Noah. "What if the rock isn't a hundred and fifty-million years old?"

The other students looked at Noah like he'd lost his

head.

"Did you know," asked Noah, "that the explorer Marco Polo said dinosaurs were alive during his time in China? He said the emperor used them to lead his carriage."

"What?" asked Noah's assistant.

"And you can go back in the history books to see that the Chinese government had a paid dragon trainer on staff."

"Yeah," said one of the other students. "And the Loch Ness Monster still lives in Scotland."

"It might," said Noah. "Did you know that America's Loch Ness Monster lives in Lake Champlain?"

"Yes," said Dr. Great. "And they say Mokele-mbembe still lives in the African Congo. But we're talking real science Noah. These are actual bones that we can find, test and study."

"Well, the only foolproof way to find something's age is for somebody to actually see it and record their findings,' said Noah. "That's more accurate than Carbon or Uranium-lead testing."

"That may be right Noah, but there's no proof that those dinosaurs recorded in history still exist," said Dr. Great.

"But," said Noah. He hesitated. He wanted to explain to everyone that dinosaurs were still alive today, he'd seen three of them. But they'd all think he was crazy. They wouldn't believe him.

"Wait a sec," said Noah. "What's in the African Congo?"

"Mokele-mbembe," said Dr. Great. "It's supposed to be a long-necked dinosaur about the size of an elephant. But like Champ in Lake Champlain, there hasn't been any solid evidence to prove they exist. Until something solid appears

Noah, something we can test and study, I'll have a hard time believing they're real."

Noah opened his mouth like he was going to reply, then he shut it. He continued to dig in the dirt, wiping away all the bones to see what they revealed. "I can't wait to tell my family about this dinosaur," he said.

"Don't worry," said Dr. Great. "We'll take lots of pictures of you and your Camarasaurus."

CHAPTER 7
NATHAN AND PROFESSOR WILL

"You know Nathan, you're really good at giving people tours at this museum," said Professor Will. "But I'd like you to be more careful about sharing your dinosaur experience."

Prof. Will and Nathan had each grabbed a soda and sat down in the foyer after the recent visitors disappeared. Things had slowed down and there were currently no visitors to tour. There were always quiet times like this in the day. Usually Prof. Will would sit and work in his office, but today he decided to have a seat with Nathan.

"Yeah, I know," said Nathan. "That man and his son

really got spooked after I opened my big, fat mouth."

"They certainly did," said Prof. Will. "But I know that seeing what you saw was a big deal. It would be a big deal for anybody. The only problem is that most people are going to doubt what you say. You could tell them the moon was made from Swiss cheese and it wouldn't make a difference. They don't know how to handle that kind of information."

"Yeah, you're right," said Nathan. "Those guys were really learning something too. They totally changed after I told them about Champ."

Prof. Will leaned forward and looked at Nathan. "You gave them too much information," he said.

"What do you mean?" asked Nathan.

"People can only digest so much new information. I know that sounds silly, but it's kind of like eating your favorite pizza. It tastes great when you're eating it, but once your stomach is full, things change. Keep eating on a full stomach and you'll get sick. You'll puke all over the place because your belly can't handle that much food!"

Nathan teased, "Yeah, especially if it's anchovies!"

"Hey," said Prof. Will. "I like anchovies."

"You do?" asked Nathan.

"Yes," said Prof. Will. "They're very tasty!"

"I'll take your word for it," said Nathan.

Prof. Will smiled at him. "The mind is a lot like your stomach. You can learn a lot of new information, but you can't do it all in one sitting. If you do, your mind will get so stuffed that it throws out everything it was just taught."

"Yeah, you're right," said Nathan.

"Those guys learned a lot from you!" said Prof. Will.

"But the thought that dinosaurs still live today, that was too hard for them to believe. Your experience is something that doesn't happen to many people. Those visitors are used to everyday life as they know it. To imagine that dinosaurs still live today, well that's hard for them to believe. Their brains couldn't handle it."

"Yeah," said Nathan. "I guess you're right. I just get so excited about Champ."

"I would too!" said Prof. Will. "But Nathan, these people have been taught all of their lives that dinosaurs died millions of years ago. It takes time to change that thought in their head. You did a great job sharing with them true science, but they rejected it all when you mentioned you saw dinosaurs last year."

The two sat for a few moments, staring at the displays in the museum lobby.

"You know," said Nathan, "my Uncle Jim told me people thought he was crazy too. He's seen Champ, several times actually, but he doesn't tell many people about it. I think he almost didn't tell us! I guess he worried we'd think he was crazy."

"I wouldn't want my family thinking I'm crazy," said Prof. Will. "It's bad enough when a stranger thinks you're crazy."

"No kidding," said Nathan. "I don't blame Uncle Jim. I think my Dad doesn't believe him. That'd be tough to have a brother that doesn't believe you. I have enough trouble with my brother. I can't imagine how bad we'd be if he thought I was crazy too."

"Well," said Prof. Will, "he probably thinks you're crazy

anyway. Most brothers do. Shoot, I think you're crazy."

Prof. Will slapped Nathan on the knee and laughed. Nathan looked offended, but then realized Prof. Will was joking. The two sat and drank their sodas for a bit.

"I'm not crazy though," said Nathan. "I really did see Champ and her babies."

"I believe you," said Prof. Will.

"You do?" asked Nathan.

"Of course I do!" said Prof. Will. "I've heard too many stories from people to doubt yours. Being in this field, I hear a lot of things from sincere and honest people! It seems, when people realize that evolution isn't real, they start to wonder what else isn't real. Why, just yesterday somebody told me they saw Bigfoot."

"Really?" asked Nathan.

"Yes!" said Prof. Will. "I hear stuff all the time! Why, even your own mother saw something when she was a little girl in the Congo."

"Mom? In the Congo?" asked Nathan. "What are you talking about?"

"Oh," said Prof. Will. "You don't know? Well, then it's not my place to tell you about it. But maybe you should ask her if she ever saw anything while she was on the mission field in the Congo."

"Really?" asked Nathan. "Cool, I will! No wonder she doesn't doubt our seeing Champ. Dad doesn't believe it at all, but Mom does. She doesn't think we're silly."

The two sat a bit longer and drank from their sodas.

"That's really cool," said Nathan. "I can't believe mom saw a dinosaur in the Congo."

"Now don't go saying I told you about it," said Prof. Will. "There's probably a good reason why she's never told you. I didn't mean to let it out like that. I just figured you knew. Please hang on to that with care. I don't want to hurt anything between you and your mother."

"Okay, I'll keep it secret," said Nathan. "I think it's cool, but I won't say anything."

"Well, no," said Prof. Will. "Go ahead and ask her about it. But don't go gossiping about it to everyone. Find a time when it's just you and her."

"That's really cool," said Nathan.

"What?" asked Prof. Will.

"That she saw something in the Congo! I mean, that's one of my dreams. To live in the Congo like her and my grandparents. I'd really like to be a missionary there. Mom says she loved life there. I know there wouldn't be any video games, but I think I'd like it too, and what better way to live a life than to help people know God better? But knowing there could be dinosaurs there too, man, that's a bonus! That's like both of my dreams tied up in one!"

"Both dreams?" asked Prof. Will.

"Yeah," said Nathan. "I could live for God and study dinosaurs at the same time! Maybe I could do some documentary about biblical creation and dinosaurs! Then I could try to program it into a video game, so kids could learn about it! I'll make it some kind of adventure in the Congo."

Prof. Will smiled and sipped on his drink.

"Yeah!" said Nathan. "I'll call it 'Adventure In The Congo!' You have to find and save people in the Congo before the dinosaurs eat them, or you!"

Prof. Will laughed. "You have quite an imagination."

"Oh, I'm just getting started," said Nathan. "Then if you go out at night, you'll have to face the terrible pterodactyls and even zombies!"

"Zombies," said Prof. Will. "What's that got to do with the Congo?"

"Well, you gotta have zombies in a video game," said Nathan. "We can make them dinosaur zombies. Maybe people bit by the dinosaurs become weird zombies or something. And you have to plead the blood of Jesus on them to bring them back to life!"

"Okay," said Prof. Will. "I think you're really stretching it now. Besides, how would you program video games in the Congo? You might not have any electronics, or worse, no electricity"

"I haven't gotten that far yet," said Nathan. "But I'll figure it out. Maybe it'll be more advanced by the time I grow up and get there."

"Well they better get a move on!" said Prof. Will. "It won't be many more years until you're able to go."

"That's right Congo!" said Nathan. "Get moving! Get yourself some electricity!"

Nathan and Prof. Will laughed at each other. Nathan tried to drink some more soda, but he started laughing again in the middle of the drink. The soda erupted from his nose!

"Oh yuck!" shouted Nathan.

This really tickled Prof. Will, and the two laughed some more. After a minute they calmed down and Nathan gave his nose a long blow to clear it out.

"So next week is the big week with your Uncle Jim! Are

you excited?" asked Prof. Will.

"Yes I am," said Nathan. "I'm hoping we get to see Champ again. And if nothing else, at least Uncle Jim will take us fishing and cook us a delicious dinner."

Nathan's parents were going to a week long homeschool conference that was a couple of states away. They had been to the local conference for their area before, but this one was supposed to be the Grand Daddy of conferences. There were big activities and even movie stars teaching classes. They were excited, and Nathan and Noah didn't have to go! Mom and Dad were letting them stay the week with their Uncle Jim on Lake Champlain!

In front of the museum a minivan pulled into view. It was filled with a large family and some excited looking kids. Nathan and Prof. Will threw away their sodas and got ready to talk with some new people about biblical creation.

"I'm going to miss having you around here next week," said Professor Will.

"You are?" asked Nathan.

"Yes I am!" said Prof. Will. "You've learned a lot here and you're a really big help!"

"Thanks," said Nathan. "I'm glad I can do it!"

"Why don't you greet these people and start their tour," said Prof. Will. "I'll stay back and wait to see if you need any help."

"Awesome!" said Nathan. "Thanks Prof. Will!"

CHAPTER 8
WHO'S THE JERK?

One week later Noah and Nathan were headed to meet their Uncle Jim. Their parents, John and Marie, would be taking them most of the way to Lake Champlain, because it was on the way to their big conference. Then they'd meet Uncle Jim at Mom's favorite store, SwedishHomes.

Not too long into the trip Dad stopped at a gas station to get a soda for everyone in the car. It was a special road-trip-treat because the Drake family didn't splurge like this everyday. Usually they shared drinks.

Everyone had a super-extra-large, except Norah. Dad ordered her a medium. She was still in diapers so bathroom stops weren't that dangerous, but a super-extra-large was just too big for a toddler. She had to have her own cup when it came to soda. If you shared a sip of your soda with her she would scream when you dared to take it back.

The splurge was nice, but Dad was already regretting buying everyone their own. His high hopes for a quick trip were quickly being dashed by Nathan's bladder. They had already stopped on the side of the road three times so Nathan could relieve himself. It didn't seem like he would be done anytime soon.

Norah was now two years old but she'd correct you if you called her that age. "I'm not two, I almost tree!" She was sassy, but still cute. Her two older brothers seemed to encourage this behavior because they were always defending her. The neighbors said she was "trouble with protection," meaning she could do what she wanted and her brothers would keep her from problems.

Norah would be joining the boys on their stay with Uncle Jim. Noah and Nathan weren't excited about this, but they were used to it by now. A week without their parents was exciting, but having their sister in tow meant they'd still have responsibility. That was okay. Since she was so young, nearly three, they could still have a guys' week with their uncle.

There was one potential problem with the upcoming week. Noah was still not getting along with Nathan. Even after the recent time away, because of the dinosaur dig, they still weren't getting along.

The current rift started when Noah was recounting the recent dig. It was probably the tenth time he had told the story to his parents, but he was so excited he couldn't help himself. He was even featured on the front cover of a "Kids 4 Creation" magazine because of the Camarasaurus find. The magazine did a full feature on Noah, the discovery, and his thoughts on the age of the dinosaur.

Noah thought everyone would be excited for him, but Nathan wasn't. Noah had been telling everyone about how the dinosaur was one of the best finds to date when Nathan interrupted.

"Did I tell you that I told a guy at the Creation Museum about Champ?" asked Nathan.

"I'm sorry, what?" asked Noah.

"Champ," said Nathan. "I told someone at the museum about how we saw her."

"Are you serious?" asked Dad. "Why? What'd they say?"

"They didn't say anything," said Nathan. "I think it scared them. They left the museum not long after I mentioned I'd seen a dinosaur."

"As exciting as that may have been for you Nathan, I was still talking," said Noah.

"You're always talking," said Nathan. "You've told us about the Camarasaurus probably a million times. I'm tired of hearing about it."

"Well," said Noah, "I'm sorry something so exciting happened to me. It's not my fault you weren't able to qualify to go."

"You're a real jerk Noah," said Nathan. "Who would want to go with you anyway?"

"You're a jerk," said Noah.

"That's enough," said Dad. "You're both being jerks."

"Can't you go one hour without talking about how cool and smart you are?" asked Nathan.

"I said that's enough!" said Dad. He looked at Mom with concern. "You two haven't been getting along since your last visit with Uncle Jim. What's going on?"

"I don't know," said Noah. "It's not my fault Nathan didn't have a good spring break."

"I did have a good break!" said Nathan. "I got to serve at the Creation Museum! It was fun, but I'm not sure about this week with you."

"Nathan," said Dad. "Give me your soda. I want you to sit and look out the window. No talking for 10 minutes. Do you think you can do that?"

Nathan didn't answer, but he nodded. He knew his Dad couldn't see him, but he stubbornly kept his mouth shut.

"I said do you think you can do that?" asked Dad.

"I nodded yes," said Nathan.

That made Dad mad. He turned the rearview mirror so he could see Nathan and gave him the evil eye. He was about to say something when Mom put her hand on his leg.

"Let it go honey," she said. "He'll be quiet."

The car was quiet as a library now. All three guys were fuming and keeping quiet. The girls just looked out the window. Norah began to sing in the silence.

"Yes, Jesus loves me," sang Norah. "Yes, Jesus loves me. Yes Jesus." These were the only words she remembered in the song, but it was still cute.

Nathan dug in his backpack and pulled out a video game. He tapped away at the buttons and Noah heard a dinosaur roar. That meant he was playing Dinsoaur Farm, his old favorite.

Last year Nathan hadn't had his own personal video game system. Noah had always shared with him. It caused a lot of arguments between the two, but it worked for a while. This year Nathan got his own system for his birthday. He had been so excited. Noah was too, it meant he didn't have to give up his game time or worry about Nathan breaking his system. But something seemed to change. Noah saw a big difference in Nathan's attitude. Was it pride? It was almost as if Nathan thought having his own system made him better than Noah. Noah didn't like that thought. He worked hard, possibly harder than Nathan, for everything he wanted. It seemed like Nathan was given a lot of things Noah had to work for.

Noah had battled with these thoughts a lot in the last year. They constantly came back to his mind and he'd have to fight them off so he could do everyday tasks. He needed a distraction. His book! He had checked out the library book about Champ that he had read last summer. Since he was going to the lake he thought it'd be fun to re-read some of the old tales about Champ. Nathan grabbed the book from his backpack and began to read.

"Champ is the name locals gave to a dinosaur-like monster that legends say lives in Lake Champlain. People report sightings of it every year. Most folks think Champ is a plesiosaur, or a dinosaur with flippers. The lake monster is usually thought to be about twenty feet long, or as long as a small school bus. In 2015, two women on wave runners had the opportunity to see Champ. "We saw Champ's

head moving across the water, about 50 feet away. We first thought it was somebody swimming in the deep part of the water. We kept watching because we were worried about their safety. After a minute we realized it wasn't human, and it had to be Champ! The monster's head was attached to a long body and it made swirling waves as it swam across the water. It finally sank below the surface. The swirling waves continued for a bit and then the water became smooth as glass."

Noah put the book down and looked at his brother Nathan. He and Nathan had seen Champ almost a year ago, when they had visited their Uncle Jim. He was hoping to see her again. He also hoped the fighting with his brother could be put on hold while they had their guys' week together. He and Nathan had always gotten along before. Maybe, for now, they could get along and have a good week.

Nathan looked up. He noticed Noah had been staring at him. "What?" he whispered.

Noah shrugged his shoulders and Nathan scowled at him. Then Nathan whispered again. "I gotta go again."

Noah couldn't resist laughing to himself. "Stop drinking so much!"

"But it's so good," said Nathan. The two boys smiled at each other.

CHAPTER 9
MEETING UNCLE JIM

Several hours later the Drake family finally arrived at their meeting spot, SwedishHomes. It was a huge warehouse that sold furniture and kitchen stuff. They also had an in-house buffet with all the hot dogs and meatballs you could want.

Uncle Jim hadn't arrived yet, so the family strolled through the store like a bunch of tourists. They didn't have a SwedishHomes where they lived, so it was always a treat to visit one. Plus the boys were always allowed to buy something cool, as long as it wasn't too expensive.

Both boys found treasures they had to have. Noah got a

GPS tracker that doubled as a pocket knife. It could be used if you got lost, or if you just needed to cut something open. Nathan got a guide book to his favorite video game, dinosaur farm. It had special directions on how to earn new and exotic dinosaur gear. Norah found something she had to have too. It was an extra-large pack of plastic dinosaur toys.

"Wow," said Noah. "There must be twenty dinosaurs in there! Look, here's a Camarasaurus! That's what I found in Utah."

"Wow," said Nathan. "He's got a big head too! Just like Noah's!"

Marie Drake immediately interrupted the conversation and grabbed the pack of plastic dinosaurs. "These are perfect!" she said. "Now you have something to play with this week."

Norah beamed. "Camera store," she said, pointing at the bag.

"Good job," said Noah. "It's a Camarasaur." It looked like she too was walking in his footsteps with a love for dinosaurs.

"John," said Marie, "Why don't you take Norah to the bathroom and change her diaper?"

"Already?" asked John. "I changed her when we got here!"

"Yes honey," said Marie. She opened her eyes extremely wide and spoke to John slowly, through a fake smile. "You need to give her a new one!" Marie was trying to tell John, without saying it out loud, to give her a minute with the boys. John didn't get it though.

"Can't it wait until we check out?" asked John.

"No John," said Marie. "She needs one now." Marie picked up Norah and placed her in John's arms.

"I need die-pee now Dada," said Norah.

John smiled at Norah and then looked at Marie in confusion. He took a deep breath and grabbed the diaper bag. "Come on Norah, let's give your mom some more time to shop."

"I need die-pee Dada," said Norah.

"I know, I know," said John. He and Norah walked ahead of Noah, Nathan and their Mom. Marie immediately turned around and crouched low to speak to the boys in a quiet voice.

"I am tired of this constant fighting," she said. "Whatever is going on between you two, I want you to get it straightened out this week."

"Nothing's going on Mom," said Noah.

"Yes it is," said Marie. "Nathan just told you you've got a big head."

"He does," said Nathan in a whiny voice.

"That's enough," said Marie. "His head is just as big as yours. I don't know what's gotten into you two, but it's done. You're brothers and you're best friends. It's time to act like it. You get this stuff out of your system and have a good week together. Okay?"

The boys looked at each other like they didn't want to agree with Marie.

"I said Okay?" repeated Marie, glaring at the two of them.

Nathan took a deep breath and said, "Okay Mom."

"Okay," repeated Noah.

Marie glared at them a bit longer. Then she took a breath and said, "Okay, it's done."

Both boys nodded. Marie stood up and looked at the two of them. "I love you boys. You're better than this petty bickering. It's time to act like it."

Both boys nodded again.

"Now let's see if we can find anything else we've got to have while we're here. We don't get to visit SwedishHomes very often. Let's enjoy it while we can."

The boys and their mom continued shopping. John and Norah eventually returned from the bathroom and joined them. It seemed like they stayed at SwedishHomes for an eternity. Sometimes shopping drags on like that, but finally their Uncle Jim called to let them know that he had arrived. The family hurried to the registers to check out. Then they met Uncle Jim at the storefront eatery for some hot dogs and soda.

Uncle Jim looked at the kids with his mouth wide open in amazement. "I can't believe how much you've grown!" exclaimed Uncle Jim. He gave each boy a bear hug and then picked up Norah for a squeeze.

"I almost tree!" said Norah.

"My goodness," said Uncle Jim. "You'll be a teenager before long!"

"Yep!" said Norah proudly. "Then I have babies like Mom!"

Everyone laughed.

"No," said Mom grinning. "You need to wait a long time to have kids."

"I want be like Mom!" said Norah.

"You're so cute!" said Uncle Jim.

"Yep!" said Norah smiling.

"And you know it too," said Uncle Jim.

"Yeah," said Norah.

Uncle Jim placed Norah on the ground and kneeled down beside her. "Do you want to come stay a week at the lake with me?" he asked.

"Yes!" exclaimed Norah. "I'll catch the big fish!" she said.

"Oh no you don't," said Noah. "I'm going to get the big one this time."

"Not on your life," said Nathan. "We all know I'm the best fisherman."

"Okay, okay," said Uncle Jim. "That's enough bragging. We can all have some fun without the big competition. Besides," he smiled, "there's no way you'll get a bigger fish than me!"

All three kids jumped up with their reply. The competition was on! Nathan even faked a kick, like he was going to kick Uncle Jim in the behind. Unfortunately he lost his balance and fell backwards. Everyone laughed, even Nathan.

Uncle Jim helped him back to his feet and asked, "What did I get myself into?"

"Oh there's no backing out now," said Marie. "It's too late for that! Besides, we have a conference to get to."

"That's right!" said John. "We've got speakers to listen to and curriculum to buy!"

"Scaredy cats," said Uncle Jim.

"I don't know," said John. "A trip to the lake sounds like

more fun than a homeschool conference."

"You didn't say that yesterday," said Marie, knocking her husband on the shoulder. "You were pretty excited about it then." In a mock voice she said, "I can't wait to see Christian Star! That's what you said last night!" Then mocking again she said, "He's the coolest!"

"He is cool," said John grinning sheepishly. "Even if he does have a funny name, but you have to admit that it's hard to beat a week at the lake!"

"How about a week with your wife?" Marie asked in a stern voice.

"Yeah, you got me there," said John. "A week with my wife wins every time."

"That's what I thought," said Marie smiling.

John gave her a kiss on the cheek.

"You two are so cute," said Uncle Jim in admiration. "Even after all these years. You have such a great family."

"That's because we know when we need to get away, just the two of us, and take a break," said John. "Thanks so much for taking the kids this week."

"Yes," said Marie. "There's no way we could do this conference with the kids. You're a life saver Jim."

"Well," said Uncle Jim, "I know how much fun the kids had last time. I'm sure this time will be even better because there aren't any criminals poaching at the lake."

"Thank God for that," said John.

"Can I get a witness?" teased Marie.

"And listen," said Uncle Jim. "If you have any worries, just give me a call. I've got a new phone with a good signal on the lake. I'll keep it by my side so you can call anytime."

"Oh, I almost forgot!" said Marie. "Boys, you got an email from Frankie Slaughter!"

"We did?" asked Noah.

"Yes," said Marie. "It came in the night before we left. I would have told you sooner, but I forgot."

"Cool," said Nathan. "I was wondering when he'd write back."

"What did he say?" asked Noah.

"Well, I don't know," said Marie. "I was in such a hurry that I didn't read it, but I did print you a copy! I packed it in your bag."

CHAPTER 10
FRANKIE'S LETTER

Several hours later Noah, Nathan, Norah and Uncle Jim were getting closer and closer to Lake Champlain. Since he'd never had kids, Uncle Jim didn't realize the unwritten rule about large sodas on road trips. Jim Drake thought, like his brother, he'd have fun and treat the kids to some sodas and sweets. The sweets disappeared quickly, only to be replaced by short-term tummy aches that the kids tried to wash away with swigs of soda. That end result was a lot of bathroom visits.

Jim was more patient than his brother, probably because he wasn't used to having kids every hour of every day. He made all the necessary bathroom stops, though he seemed to quickly realize that additional drinks would have to wait until the end of the trip.

Uncle Jim had tried to spoil the kids with some new DVDs for the television in his SUV. Norah had to have the girly one first, but she quickly fell asleep and the boys pounced on the latest action movie that had just been released.

The movie was about a mysterious island that had been found and it was loaded with fire-breathing dragons. The dragons had trapped a family of six inside an old RV on the island. They were spewing fire at the trailer to make it hotter than an oven inside. In the end one of the kids was able to save the day by feeding the dinosaurs bubble gum. Somehow the gum made their teeth stick together so they couldn't spit flames anymore.

"That's so silly," said Nathan. "Bubble Gum would never work to make your mouth stick together. At least try something that's real. Maybe peanut butter, like when you stick it to the roof of a dog's mouth."

"Peanut butter could work," said Uncle Jim. "Those T-rex's arms are so small they couldn't wipe it away. They'd be licking that peanut butter off for hours!"

The movie credits rolled and the boys looked for a deleted scene at the end of the credits. Sure enough, a clip appeared with a ferocious looking dinosaur rising up from the ocean. It was near the statue of liberty in New York City. The monster looked left, then right, and then sank beneath the water. Suddenly it jumped back up and spit flames at the TV screen. The boys hadn't expected the

80

surprise and it made them both jump.

"Cool!" said Nathan, spilling some soda on his lap. "The next movie is about Leviathan!"

"That is cool," said Noah, "You know, one of my favorite creation teachers says the Leviathan could have been the T-rex. He says it could have been a fire-breathing dragon."

"Really?" asked Nathan. "I've never heard that before. How could it be the T-rex?"

"Because its head is larger than it should be for its body size," said Noah "Plus there's a large empty space inside its skull. That empty space could be a place where chemicals were stored to create fire."

"That's interesting," said Uncle Jim. "That's kind of like that one beetle. What's it called? Oh yeah, the bombardier beetle. Have you heard of the bombardier beetle?"

"No, does it spit fire?" asked Nathan.

"No, not fire," said Uncle Jim. "It squirts chemicals from its backside to burn its enemies. The chemicals could kill the beetle if they were mixed together inside its belly, so they're separated while inside. It's no big deal while they're separate, but watch out when the beetle attacks. It squirts those chemicals, mixing them together during the attack. The reaction from the mixture is so hot that it scalds anything nearby!"

"So," asked Nathan, "you think a T-rex could have done the same thing?"

"Maybe so," said Noah. "It would simply need a little something extra to light the chemicals on fire."

"Maybe that's how Dad gets so mad when he sees we don't do our chores," said Nathan.

"A fire-breathing Dad?" Noah asked, laughing. "He's never breathed fire at me."

"Well, he just needs that extra chemical reaction," joked Nathan. "But sometimes it's like a switch is flipped and he gets mad at me! Maybe that's some kind of chemical reaction."

"Yeah, watch out," said Uncle Jim. "You just need something to ignite the anger and he'll be spitting fire!"

The boys and Uncle Jim all laughed for a minute.

"But Mom doesn't breathe fire," said Nathan. "She's too nice."

"Oh yes she does," said Uncle Jim. "I've seen her spit fire at your father several times! You just haven't made her mad enough!"

Noah imagined his mom breathing fire at his dad because there wasn't enough soda for the road trip. "Yeah," he said in agreement. "I guess that could happen."

"Speaking of your Mom," said Uncle Jim. "What did that letter from Frankie say?"

"Oh my gosh," Noah said. "I forgot to read it! Mom said it's in my book bag." Noah dug in his bag and pulled out the letter for everyone to see.

"Could you read it out loud?" asked Nathan.

"Sure!" said Noah. He opened the letter, cleared his throat and began to read.

Hey guys! Thank you so much for giving me a Bible and keeping our email friendship going! You really have helped to change my life. I never knew there could be somebody so loving as you, and then I met Jesus too! Awesome!

While reading the Bible I decided I wanted to be less selfish. You know, I don't want to think only about myself and my desires. I've been trying to think about others and how I can help them! Did you know that even in prison I can help people out? Well, not out, like out of jail. But I can help people to show them the love of Christ!

The other day I helped the prison guard. He'd been having trouble from some prisoners in the yard. Know what I did? I walked over to those knuckle-heads and told them to shape up or I'd bash their heads in. It worked! Those dummies changed their behavior and started being good. The prison guard even thanked me for helping! I can totally do this helping, unselfish thing!

I've also been trying to work more diligently. For example, I'm trying to do the best work that I can at a laundry job they gave me. It's really paying off, literally! I found ten dollars in a pair of some inmate's pants!

I'm sorry I haven't written for a while. I've been meaning to. I'm writing now, because I need your help. I know of a bad situation and there's nothing I can do about it. I don't know who I can tell to try to help fix it. My hope is that you might be able to do something with this information. Maybe you can get it to your Uncle Jim!

Uncle Jim spoke up, "Well that's convenient! What is it?"

"Let's see," said Noah. He continued to read.

As you know, my Grandpa Edwin really wants to capture that old dinosaur named Champ! Grandpa wants to make Champ some kind of trophy-catch. He thinks it will somehow honor my Great Grandpa, Sammy. You know, restore honor to his name.

Well, Grandpa is still on the search for Champ. I figured he would give up and lay low so he could stay out of jail. I was wrong. He came to my prison today and offered to break me out. I couldn't believe he'd do such a thing. I mean, in the past I would have probably accepted his offer. But now that I know the difference between right and wrong, I told him no way! It may be tempting, but I bet he'd get me into more trouble anyway.

I know Grandpa is serious though. In fact, he's more serious now than ever before. He even helped break my older brother, Seth, out of jail! This is very bad news! Grandpa is kind of harmless when he's alone. You know, he's a feeble, old man! But now he's stirring up trouble with a known criminal! Seth was in jail for trying to kill a couple of guys. He's very bad, and unlike me, he's only interested in himself. I can't believe Grandpa would even consider getting help from Seth! This means that Grandpa is really, really desperate. I guess he feels like there's nowhere else to turn for help. Too bad he doesn't have Jesus!

Listen, I don't want to put you guys in harm's way. I've put you through enough. I just thought I'd let you know because maybe your uncle and the local police can step in to solve the problem. Maybe they can do something to protect Champ and her babies. Maybe they can do something to put Grandpa away and make sure Seth is caught.

I'm so sorry to burden you with this problem, but you're the only ones that I know and trust. Besides, there's more help in bigger numbers! It's like the Bible says in Ecclesiastes 4:9-12:

"Two are better than one, because they have a good reward for their labor. For if they fall, the one will lift up his fellow; but woe to him who is alone when he falls, and doesn't have another to lift him up."

Noah and Nathan, right now you are the only ones that I trust. You guys are so awesome. I hope you can do something to help

Champ! I will be praying for you. Love in Christ, Frankie.

Nathan and Noah looked at each other.

"Grandpa Edwin is back!" said Nathan.

"And we have to help!" said Noah.

"No, the local police have to help," said Uncle Jim. "We have to relax and enjoy our time together! You kids can't get into any more trouble. Thank God your parents didn't read this letter! You'd be on your way to a homeschool conference if they had!"

"Yeah," said Noah. "Maybe we should keep this to ourselves for now."

"Well," said Uncle Jim, "we could keep it to ourselves and the local police! Can you imagine if your mother had found out? She'd be spitting fire!"

CHAPTER 11
EDWIN AND SETH

Somewhere on a highway in Vermont an old sports car drove westbound towards Lake Champlain. Inside, the radio was playing country music.

"We're tearing down this highway, tearing down this highway. We got some real nice wheels, got some real nice wheels. The cops are on the lookout, cops are on the lookout. They don't like how we deal, don't like how we deal. I guess it don't matter, guess it don't matter. We got more we can steal, got more we can steal. Cause we're like Bonnie and Clyde, Bonnie and Clyde, on the run to save our hide."

The song came to a close and a local news report took its place. The news anchor lead with the story of an escaped convict. "Police are still on the lookout for a notorious criminal that could be headed to Lake Champlain."

A loud snore overpowered the news anchor's voice. Seth Slaughter was sleeping. His grandfather, Edwin, was driving. Edwin rolled his eyes and hit Seth on the arm. "Be quiet, I can't hear the news!" He reached to the radio and turned up the volume. Seth Slaughter sat up and shielded his eyes from the noonday sun.

The news anchor continued his report. "Seth Slaughter had been serving time for attempted manslaughter because he nearly killed two business partners over a management dispute. Slaughter escaped during a routine transfer to a prison in South Burlington, jumping into an old Packard Hawk sports car. Slaughter didn't leave without injury. He was shot in the foot during the getaway. Police believe he will be limping, if he is walking at all. Authorities add that he is armed and dangerous because he stole an officer's handgun.

"Slaughter may be traveling with his grandfather, Edwin, who is also wanted for charges of kidnapping and theft. Edwin and his classic Packard Hawk car were last seen at a prison in Waterbury, Vermont. They were visiting another family member in jail. Officers suspect no jail breaks in Waterbury. In fact, they believe Seth and Edwin Slaughter could be headed to Lake Champlain..."

Edwin Slaughter turned the radio off. "Well, we've made the headlines!"

"Yeah, that's a good way to lay low," said Seth. He was

really laying on the sarcasm. "Good thing we're driving the same car the police are looking for!"

"I know," said Grandpa Edwin. "Maybe we should pull over somewhere and drive at night."

"That would work," said Seth. "We could also find a car lot and trade out this old car for something better."

"I'm not trading this car for anything," said Edwin. "This is a good car and I've had it forever!"

"Well, I'm just saying," said Seth.

"Well don't say it anymore," said Grandpa Edwin. "Here, here's a good looking place."

The car exited the highway at a lonely looking overpass. Except for a sign that pointed to civilization twenty miles away, there was no sign of life.

Seth crossed his left leg onto his lap and slowly pried his shoe off. He'd been taking it off a lot because of the bullet hole in his foot. Underneath the shoe was a hefty wrap of cotton gauze, some of it stained red from the wound.

Edwin stopped the car at the top of the overpass and watched Seth baby his foot. Seth carefully unwrapped the gauze and set it in his shoe. Then he probed the wound with his finger, checking to make sure everything was all right. "Ow," he said to himself a few times. "Ow!" The bullet had gone in between Seth's big and second toes, right through the shoe. Amazingly, no bones had been broken, but there was a good chunk of toe missing. Seth didn't bother going to a hospital. He would have gone straight back to jail. He was lucky though. He would have needed medical attention if the wound had been any worse.

Suddenly Seth realized the car wasn't moving. He

looked up and noticed Grandpa Edwin staring at him. "What?" he asked.

Edwin huffed a deep sigh and continued to drive.

"What's the problem?" asked Seth.

"You keep checking that bullet wound, like it's going to be better," said Edwin. "You need to keep it wrapped so it can heal, and so the car won't stink so bad. Even with the windows open, your feet stink!"

Seth tried to ignore his grandpa. He looked at the bullet wound a bit more. After a moment he seemed satisfied and wrapped it back up in the cotton gauze. But he decided to leave his shoe off for the rest of the afternoon.

"We'll find us a lonely looking grove of trees and park in the shade," said Grandpa Edwin. He continued driving down a road that was infested with pot holes.

Seth pulled a smart phone from his pocket and began to tap on the screen. He had stolen the phone during a bathroom break at a gas station. He was so excited to find it. He'd never had a smart phone before, just flip phones. Smart phones weren't popular until after Seth was thrown in jail.

"Dog gone Gramps, we must still be in the middle of nowhere! I can't seem to get any internet on this phone!"

"Internet? What do you need internet for?" asked Grandpa Edwin.

"I don't know," said Seth. "This game says it won't play without an internet connection. Things sure have changed since I was in prison. Phones didn't even play video games back then."

Grandpa Edwin laughed, "Have you really been in jail

that long?"

"I guess so," said Seth. "Smart phones weren't this smart when I started my time. We were still getting the hang of ringtones then, forget about picture-chat and Facetube live!"

Seth punched up the camera and held out his arm like he was taking a selfie. Instead of taking a picture, he started recording a video.

"Hi, Seth Slaughter here," Seth said speaking to the camera. "I'm in the middle of nowhere. I may be somewhere by the time you see this video, but who knows."

"You gotta be kidding me," said Edwin Slaughter in shock.

Seth pointed the camera at his grandfather and said, "No, I'm not kidding Gramps. I might as well try shooting video."

"Put that thing away you dummy!" said Grandpa Edwin.

"Oh take it easy Gramps," said Seth. "This ain't gonna hurt us. I can post it to Facetube and the cops still won't catch us! We're too smart. They'll be stuck in all the wrong places anyway." Turning the camera back at himself, Seth continued, "I bet you cops are still looking for us in Vermont! You'll never find us. New York, Orlando, St. Louis, who knows where we'll be by the time you see this. We could even be in Mexico!"

"You and your brother Frankie," said Grandpa Edwin, "you two are both dummies."

"Yeah, I love you too Gramps," said Seth. Then in a mock whisper he said, "You know who's the real dummy? It's this guy right here." He pointed at Grandpa Edwin. "He thinks there's some dinosaur living in the bottom of Lake

Champlain!"

"I don't think there's one there," said Grandpa. "I know there's one there! Actually I know there's at least three there!"

"Here we go," said Seth, talking to the camera. "There's gonna be six of them by the time you watch this video."

Edwin ignored the comment. He slowed the car down and turned onto a dirt road. He continued driving, but now it was a slow crawl.

"You know what?" said Seth. "My grandpa's a spook. I like him though, he's helped me out of some tough spots. It's just that he comes from a different time. In Grandpa's day they didn't learn about things like evolution."

"Oh, I'm not that old," said Grandpa Edwin. "I'm sure evolution has been taught since the eighteen-hundreds, ever since that dummy Charles Darwin observed birds that he thought evolved."

"I thought they didn't teach that when you were a kid," said Seth.

"Oh they taught it," said Grandpa Edwin. "They just didn't shove it down our throats. Times have changed though. Schools have changed. Even the government's changed! You know, this whole evolution thing really took off in the nineteen-sixties because of the government. It was all because of the space race."

"Say what?" asked Seth, pointing the camera at Edwin Slaughter.

"Ahh, you don't know your history!" said Grandpa Edwin. "It was in the nineteen-sixties when Russia launched the first man into outer space. They were the first country to do it!"

"What's that got to do with evolution?" asked Seth.

"Well, the United States didn't want to be beat by Russia," said Grandpa Edwin. He looked at the camera and spoke really slowly like he was speaking to somebody dumb. "The United States is where we're from." Then he resumed speaking normally and said, "Our country had to be the big kid on the block. So we decided to put a man on the moon. We set our sights on being the first country to do it."

"Like I said, what's that got to do with evolution?" asked Seth.

Grandpa looked at Seth and made an aggravated snort. "Would you stop interrupting me?" He paused to wait for silence, after a moment he continued. "There were a few people in high places that wanted to change what we were teaching in school. You know, so we could catch up with Russia."

"Seriously?" asked Seth.

"Yes, seriously," said Granpda Edwin. "They figured Russia must be doing something right if they launched a man into space before we did. Anyway, a movement was started to teach some of the science that was taught in Russia. That included Evolution. Evolution was taught when I went to school, but we were also taught the Bible. All of that changed in the nineteen-sixties. Today, you have to go to a private school to learn from the Bible."

"So what?" asked Seth. "What's that got to do with Evolution?"

"You dummy," said Grandpa Edwin. "It has everything to do with Evolution! Today kids are only taught evolution in the public school system! That's all they know. They have to go somewhere else if they want to be taught anything different."

"So what?" asked Seth. "Evolution is true, not that silly Bible that you were taught from."

"Are you sure?" asked Grandpa Edwin. "Are you sure man evolved from apes? Can you prove it? I don't think you can, even though the concept has been shoved down your throat since you were a kid. Who cares if it goes against the Bible? Who cares if countries, all over, have legends about a gigantic flood that destroyed the world? Who cares if other legends talk about dragons, or other things that must have died millions of years ago?"

Grandpa Edwin stopped the car in a small grove of trees. He parked and looked at the camera. "Evolution is a closed-minded theory that was borrowed from a communist country. If evolution is true, you're nothing but a bunch of stardust from a big bang. If evolution is true then there's no point in living, except to have fun and create more humans. If evolution is true then there is no such thing as right or wrong. You're just an accident and you have no value. In fact, you're just a burden to our planet. You pollute the ecosystem and it'd be better if you were just dead!"

"Whoa Gramps," said Seth. "Take it easy! You're bringing us all down here. Nobody's gonna want to watch this video."

"Ahh, but what if evolution isn't true?!" said Grandpa Edwin. "What if a loving God made the universe and everything we know? What if we humans were created to rule and control our own little part of the world? What if we are here so that we can enjoy everything that our creator made, and then create things just like him? You know, we all have a little bit of creativity in us. After all Seth, you created your own criminal business, a chop shop for cars. God gave you that creativity! If God gave you a purpose, then you could have a life that you'd enjoy!"

"But I don't enjoy being in jail," said Seth.

"Well that's because you created something that's against the law," said Grandpa Edwin. "But Seth, God gave you an imagination just like His. He gave you the ability to create your own destiny! At least, that's what we were taught in my day. We didn't learn all this evolution mumbo-jumbo. Today the lines are so blurred, people can't tell right from wrong. We knew the difference in my day. We were taught from the Bible, and we liked it that way."

"Wow Gramps, that's some good stuff," said Seth. Turning the camera to his face he said, "and you heard it right here from Seth and Edwin Slaughter, in the middle of nowhere. In closing, I'm going to try to put this video on Facetube, if I can ever get an internet connection. I want to open up the invitation for you police officers to try to catch me and Grandpa Edwin. Go ahead and try, but you won't succeed! You know why?" He looked at his grandpa Edwin and said with a smile, "because I'm creative, and God made me that way!" He laughed, and then said, "You'll never catch me coppers!"

CHAPTER 12
A MONSTROUS CATCH

The next day Noah, Nathan and Norah woke up from a night of peaceful rest. The three kids and their Uncle Jim had slept inside a giant tent, at a campground, just uphill from Lake Champlain. It was Uncle Jim's favorite spot. It was a little off the beaten path so they wouldn't run into tourists, or potential criminals like Edwin and Seth Slaughter.

Noah sat up and looked around. His brother Nathan and sister Norah were still sleeping. The sunlight was shining onto the top of the tent. It looked as if the sun were already high in the sky.

"Wow," Noah said to himself. "We must have really slept in!"

The Drake kids did have a good excuse. They'd been in the car the whole day before, that will wear anyone out.

Noah unzipped his sleeping bag and then dug into a travel bag for some shorts and a shirt. He began to get dressed when he heard Uncle Jim's voice from outside the tent.

"Are you finally waking up?" Uncle Jim asked.

"I am," said Noah. "What time is it?"

"You've been sleeping the day away," said Uncle Jim. "It's already ten-thirty!"

"Wow," said Noah. "Thanks for letting us sleep!" He buttoned his shorts and slipped on a shirt. By now he had disturbed Nathan and Norah enough to wake them up too. Nathan was rubbing his eyes, but he didn't get up. Instead he turned over and tried to ignore the noise. Norah awoke instantly. She still had sleep in her eyes, but she was ready to go after a long night's rest.

She looked at Noah and said, "I catch big fish today!"

"You will?" asked Noah in mock surprise. "What if I catch the big fish today?"

"No," said Norah firmly. "I catch big fish. You catch Champ."

Noah laughed. His sister was so young, but she was so smart. "Okay Norah, you catch the big fish."

"Okay," said Norah. "And you catch Champ."

"How about I just catch some pictures of Champ? Do you think we could do that?" he asked.

"Yes!" said Norah. "And then show Daddy!"

"I like the way you think," said Noah. "But I'm still not sure he'd believe Champ is real, even with pictures he can see."

"Daddy believe me," said Norah.

"Maybe he would," said Noah. "Maybe he would."

Noah helped Norah put some clothes on while Nathan pretended to sleep. When she was fully dressed, the two joined Uncle Jim outside.

"I cooked up some breakfast while you were sleeping," said Uncle Jim. "Biscuits and gravy. The biscuits are cold, but the gravy is thick and warm. I think you'll enjoy it."

"Oh that's wonderful," said Noah. "Biscuits and gravy are great."

Suddenly, there was a great fuss inside the tent. Nathan hollered, "Ouch!" Then the whole tent leaned to one side and back to the other.

"Is everything all right in there?" asked Uncle Jim.

"Oh yeah," said Nathan, sticking his head out from the tent. He stepped outside and was fully clothed. "Good morning! Did somebody say biscuits and gravy?"

"Wow," said Uncle Jim. "You get dressed fast!"

"Oh yeah," said Nathan. "I move for biscuits and gravy."

"And you move the tent too!" said Uncle Jim, laughing.

Nathan blushed a little and said, "Sorry, I stepped on one of Norah's dinosaurs and tripped!"

"Have a nice trip?" asked Noah with mocked concern. "See you next fall!"

"Yeah like I haven't heard that one before," said Nathan.

"I know," said Noah. "Probably twenty minutes ago!"

Everyone giggled at that jab. Even Norah thought it was

funny. She smiled at Nathan.

The family sat down to eat. There was a lot of food but Noah and Nathan quickly cleaned it up. Norah had her fill too, of course.

"Wow," said Uncle Jim. "I thought that'd be enough for two meals! You kids really eat a lot."

"Wellf…" said Nathan. He was speaking slowly through a biscuit-packed mouth, "this if… ow favrit, breakfuff."

Noah nodded in agreement.

"I was thinking about fishing first thing this morning," said Uncle Jim. "It's a bit later than I expected, but we could still get a nice catch."

"I catch big fish today," said Norah.

"You might," said Uncle Jim. "You caught the biggest fish last time, you might do it again!"

"Yep," said Norah. "I do again!"

Uncle Jim laughed.

"By the way," said Uncle Jim. "I called the local police about Frankie Slaughter's letter. Apparently they already know about Edwin and Seth. Actually, every officer in the state does. There's a statewide manhunt for the two of them. It sounds pretty bad."

"Do you think we're okay?" asked Nathan. "I mean, is it okay to camp out here?"

"The police told me they thought we'd be fine," said Uncle Jim. "They don't know for sure where Edwin and Seth are."

"But Frankie said they were going to catch Champ!" said Nathan.

"That's what I told the police," said Uncle Jim. "But they

said there's no other evidence to support that. They said the Slaughters were last seen on the other side of the state. They also pointed out that, even if they were coming to Lake Champlain, it's a very big lake. The Slaughters could be anywhere."

"That's true," said Noah. "Lake Champlain is huge!"

"Okay," said Nathan. "If you think we're safe, then that's cool."

"All right," said Uncle Jim. "Then let's pick up this mess and go fishing!"

The kids helped Uncle Jim clean up breakfast and then each of them loaded up to go fishing. Noah helped Norah with her little pink pole, making sure that she wouldn't get caught on the hook. He and Nathan grabbed their own poles and Nathan picked up their dad's tackle box.

When they were ready, Uncle Jim led them on a hike to his new fishing spot.

"I found this spot just last month," said Uncle Jim. "Big Frank told me all about it. He's a retired guy who fishes this lake every day. He knows it like the back of his hand."

"Has he ever seen Champ?" asked Nathan.

"I don't know," said Uncle Jim. "I've never asked him. If anybody has, it's probably him. I do know he takes a load of fish home everyday. He's a pro. I'm sure fishing the right spot is a big part of it though!"

"And that's where we're going?" asked Nathan.

"Yes sir! It certainly is!" said Uncle Jim.

The family followed a small trail through the woods surrounding the lake. After a bit, Uncle Jim pointed out a marker. "This is where we turn to go the lake. See how that tree is bent? It kind of looks like a person bowing down."

Sure enough, a large tree towered up fifteen feet in the air, then its trunk turned and bent back towards the ground. The way the limbs grew it looked like a person bowing low before someone important.

"I see it!" said Nathan.

"I see it!" repeated Norah.

"Oh that's cool," said Noah.

"This is called The Old Gentleman," said Uncle Jim. "Trees don't normally grow this way."

"Yeah," said Nathan. "I've never seen a tree do that before."

"This is where we turn, at The Old Gentleman," said Uncle Jim. "If you keep going straight you'll hit a marina that rents boats and waverunners. If we turn left, we'll get to Big Frank's fishing spot!"

"Let's go," said Noah.

Uncle Jim turned left and led the kids through the woods. There was no trail here.

"This must be a secret spot," said Nathan. "There's so much brush, I bet nobody ever goes this way!"

"That's the point!" said Uncle Jim.

The hike continued. The kids pushed tree limbs and brush out of the way in order to keep up with Uncle Jim. He led them in a semi-straight line towards the lake, occasionally going around trees and bramble. Eventually the trees thinned out and the family came to the end of the hike. A small rocky bluff jutted out above the lake, about six feet above the surface. The overhang was shaded by nearby trees and it made the perfect spot to sit and enjoy the afternoon.

Down below, the water was crystal blue and smooth as glass. There were two fish circling around each other, just under the surface.

"This is the perfect spot to fish," said Noah.

"Yes it is!" said Uncle Jim. "Load up your bait and let's get started!"

Noah and Nathan both got their poles and baited their hooks with wriggling worms. They each tossed their lines in the water as Uncle Jim baited his and Norah's hooks. To Jim's surprise, Noah caught the first fish before he had his own hook in the water.

"There's number one!" said Noah.

"Oh it's on," said Nathan.

The two boys battled out the day to see who would win the competition. Last year Nathan had won. This year, Noah was determined not to let that happen again.

Uncle Jim tried to keep up with the boys, but he was too busy helping Norah and taking fish off everyone's lines. Norah was catching just as much fish as the boys. She was disappointed though, none of the fish were as big as she wanted.

"Where's big fish?" she asked.

"He's in here somewhere," said Uncle Jim. "Keep trying! We'll get him."

"Yeah," Norah said with determination. "We get him! He'll like my cute pink pole."

The surprise of the day came when Noah caught the big fish. It was a gigantic sturgeon and it nearly pulled him into the water. The line whirred as the fish swam away. Noah hollered for help and Uncle Jim was there in an instant.

It was a long fight. After a few minutes, as it was tugged closer into shore, the sturgeon jumped out of the water.

"Holy cow," said Noah. "That thing's huge!"

"No, it's monstrous!" said Nathan.

"It must be seven feet long," said Uncle Jim. "That's huge for a sturgeon, it's not normal." He tugged on the line for a bit and then said, "Last month I saw Champ chasing a really large sturgeon. Maybe this is the same one."

"Oh wow," said Noah. "That's cool!"

"Yeah," said Nathan. "We could use it as bait to catch Champ!"

"Well, no," said Uncle Jim. "We can't. It's an endangered species."

He teased at the line and reeled it in bit by bit. "We can catch this guy, but we're going to have to let him go."

"Let him go!" shouted Nathan. "No way, we can't do that!"

Uncle Jim almost had the sturgeon reeled in, but then the fight suddenly stopped. The fishing line went slack. Uncle Jim wound it all the way until he came to the end of the line. The hook was gone.

"Oh no," said Noah.

"I'm sorry Noah," said Uncle Jim. "The line snapped."

"Noah catch big fish?" asked Norah.

"No," said Noah. "He got away."

"I sorry Noah," said Norah.

"Oh, it's okay," said Noah. "We couldn't keep him anyway."

"That okay brudder," said Norah. She looked down and kicked a small rock into the water. "That fish was bigger than mine."

Noah smiled. "Well, there's still time Norah. You could get something bigger."

"I doubt it," Uncle Jim said under his breath.

"Yeah, I get something bigger," said Norah.

"I think that's a challenge" said Nathan. "I still have a chance to win this thing!"

"Not yet," said Noah. "I'm not done yet!"

"Yeah," said Norah. "I not done either!"

CHAPTER 13
FISH GUT STEW

Seth Slaughter was really enjoying his smart phone. Now that he was settled in a somewhat secure campsite, he was able to connect to the internet. He had posted the last video, the one he recorded in the car, to Facetube. It already had some views and even a few likes. Now, he was ready to do it again. Seth pointed his smartphone at himself and hit the button to broadcast live.

"Hey Facetubers! Welcome back! It's been some time since our last video, so I thought I'd give you a quick update on what's happening. When last we spoke, Gramps and I were in the middle of a highly secure, unknown location!

We stayed there for a bit and got some sleep. Then, once the sun went down, we hit the road! Now, we're safe at our next destination, ready to begin Grandpa Edwin's evil plan to take over the world!" He let out a laugh that sounded like an evil bad guy from a video game. "Bwa-ha, Bwa-ha, Bwa-ha-ha-ha-haaaa!"

"Seth!" hollered Grandpa Edwin. "Put that thing away!"

Seth pointed the camera at his Grandpa and said, "Take a chill pill Gramps."

Grandpa Edwin huffed and turned away from the camera.

The men had reached their destination during the dark early morning hours that morning. They were at Lake Champlain, camping at a clearing beside the lake. The sun was high in the sky and Grandpa Edwin was busy stirring a smoking concoction inside a huge, stainless steel pot. The pot sat on a grill on top of a large fire pit. Inside the pot was some kind of fish stew. It smelled horrible. So bad, in fact, that Grandpa Edwin had to keep a handkerchief tied over his face so he didn't inhale the fumes.

"It's okay," said Seth, turning the camera back to himself. "You know why? Because you'll never catch me coppers!" He laughed his maniacal laugh, "Bwa-ha-ha-ha!"

"Just keep it up boy," said Grandpa Edwin. "We'll see who's laughing last."

"Have a little faith Grandpa," said Seth. "I know what I'm doing!"

"Hardly!" said Edwin. "You just got out of jail!"

"I don't know what that's all about," Seth said to the camera. "Like that has anything to do with it!" The camera recording showed Grandpa Edwin in the background, just over Seth's shoulder. Edwin shook his head side to side as he continued working over the fire.

Seth looked back at the camera. "Anyway, before we were so rudely interrupted. Gramps is slaving away at the campfire. You see, he's cooking up a plan, literally."

Seth pointed the camera at Edwin Slaughter and said, "Tell us what you're doing there Gramps!"

Edwin looked at the camera. He let out a sigh and began to talk. "Legend says that there's a lake monster at this here lake," he said as he gestured to the lake in the background. "I'm stewing a special fish recipe that the old monster is going to love."

Seth moved the camera over the pot to reveal what was inside. It was a chunky black stew that looked gross and sticky. Smoke fumes rose above the bubbling fish goo and Seth choked on them.

Turning the camera back to himself, Seth said, "I told you he was a dummy." He gagged from the smoke and then continued. "He's cool, he's family, but he's a dummy."

"Just stick with me," said Grandpa Edwin. "You'll see who the real dummy is."

Seth rolled his eyes and pointed the camera at his Grandfather. "Tell us what's in this, uh, slop."

"This is a special recipe," said Grandpa Edwin. "It's handed down from my father Sammy Slaughter."

"I bet it is," said Seth.

"Daddy got it from the Bible," said Edwin.

"The Bible?" asked Seth.

"Yes," said Grandpa Edwin. "It's inspired by the book of

Daniel."

"Did Daniel like fishing for lake monsters?" asked Seth.

"No, you dummy," said Grandpa Edwin. "Daniel killed a great dragon in the extended version of his book in the Bible. It's in chapter 14."

"There's an extended version of the Bible?" asked Seth.

"There's a lot of versions of the Bible," said Grandpa Edwin. "Some versions include three extra chapters in the book of Daniel. Inside, Daniel kills a dragon that the Babylonians had worshipped as a god."

"That's cool," said Seth. "How'd he kill the dragon?"

"With a recipe very similar to this one," said Grandpa Edwin, pointing at the pot of fish goo on the fire. "Daniel cooked some animal fat, which the dragon loved. He then mixed it with tar and hair."

"Mmmm," said Seth. "Sounds, horrible."

Edwin laughed, "Yeah. It is horrible! Your great grandfather Sammy Slaughter made a slight change to the recipe. Instead of animal fat, we're mixing fish guts with some tar and hair."

"Why the tar and hair?" asked Seth.

"Ah," said Grandpa Edwin. "That's the part that does the work! Basically we're cooking a huge hairball. Dragons can't digest the tar and hair. On the other hand, they can't cough it up either. It's the perfect poison, the perfect way to kill them, and if they eat enough of it, they'll die!"

"Wow Gramps," said Seth. "You got it bad. Too bad there's no such thing as a dragon."

"I'm telling you there is!" said Grandpa Edwin. "I'm not crazy, and neither is your great grandfather Sammy. There's a family of dragons, lake monsters, or whatever you want to call them in this lake. They've lived here for centuries. Your great grandfather caught one. Your brother and I nearly caught another last year."

"And that's how Frankie got in jail," said Seth. "Helping you with some hair-brained scheme."

Edwin laughed. He lifted a scoop of hair from the boiling pot and said, "I guess hair-brained is a good way to put it!"

Seth turned the camera and pointed it back at himself. Over his shoulder you could still see Grandpa Edwin stirring the pot at the fire.

"You see?" said Seth. "What'd I tell you? He's a dummy. But I gotta love him! Gramps is my dummy, and he helped bust me out of jail."

While Seth was speaking a shovel shaped head, on top of a five-foot neck, lifted from the middle of the lake. The head turned and sniffed at the air.

"This kind of nonsense has been going on in my family for a long time," said Seth. "My great grandfather Sammy supposedly caught one of these lake monsters. At least, that's what we're told."

Over Seth's shoulder the long necked monster came closer to the shore. Grandpa Edwin looked up and jumped. He turned and looked at the camera. Pulling down the towel that covered his face, he smiled.

"Oh Seth," said Grandpa Edwin in a singsong voice. "What were you saying about being a dummy?"

Seth turned the camera back towards Grandpa Edwin. Then he noticed the monster that was in the lake behind him and shouted, "What in the heck is that?!"

Shaking, Seth focused his camera on the long-necked monster. "Holy Cow Grandpa!" he exclaimed. "There really is a lake monster! And it does look like a dragon, or a dinosaur. Oh my gosh, what is it?!"

"It's Champ," said Grandpa Edwin. "Well, that one is a Champ baby. The parent is much bigger."

"Holy cow!" said Seth. "You're not crazy!"

"That's right," said Grandpa Edwin. "And neither was my father Sammy."

"Aaaaahhh!" Hollered Seth in excitement. "It's really true!"

The monster on the camera no longer seemed comfortable. Because of all the noise from Seth, it turned away and sank below the water in a sea of bubbles.

Grandpa Edwin walked toward the camera and pointed it at himself. "Now look here," he said. "There really is a dragon in this lake. You just saw it for yourself. It's my intention to catch that dragon, well, at least its parent. I nearly caught it last year. This year I'll get it. Seth and I will get it! We'll reel this thing in and show it to the world. And one lucky bidder is gonna have the chance to buy it! You can put it on display or chop it up for research. Do whatever you want! But I'm gonna catch it and sell it to the highest bidder for half a million dollars! So get those checks ready people, and keep your eyes peeled for Edwin Slaughter."

Edwin pulled the towel over his mouth and nose and turned back to his pot of smoking fish guts. Seth kept the camera on his grandfather for a moment longer. He was in shock over seeing the lake monster. Finally he remembered the recording and turned the camera back towards himself.

"It really is true!" exclaimed Seth. "Champ really is in Lake Champlain!" His eyes grew wide. "Oh my gosh! I just told you where I'm at!" He grimaced and scratched his head. After thinking for a moment he shrugged his shoulders. "Oh well. I guess Lake Champlain is huge. It spans across New York, Vermont and even Quebec in Canada. That's a large area, and you know what that means? It means you'll never catch me coppers!"

Seth put the phone down to stop the recording. Then he remembered something and put it back up in a selfie position.

"Hey, listen. I need something. Maud, you're in this area. If you see this video, I need you to find me a boat. Not just a boat, I'm talking a smokin' hot yacht." Seth scratched his head. "No, that's not good. We can't draw too much attention. Tell you what, I need a nice sized boat. Maud, I need it fully loaded. You know what I mean, fully loaded? And Maud, I need it like now, right now. Thanks, I owe you big time."

Seth put the phone down and stopped the live broadcast.

CHAPTER 14
THE DELIVERY

Maud sat in her stuffy office. She hated offices. She was more of an outdoor person. When she was a child her father had spent loads of time with her outdoors. They'd hike through forests, boat across wavy lake waters and even camp under the stars at night. Maud missed those times, but they had passed a long time ago. It was another lifetime, at least that's what she told herself.

Maud was ninety-seven years old, though she didn't seem it. She was older looking of course, but she looked young for her age. The reason was because Maud didn't grow old on the inside. She still had a youthful personality about her. She stayed young because she didn't sit around twiddling her thumbs. She kept busy, very busy.

For example, a normal woman in her nineties could stay youthful by growing a garden. That's an adventure for someone in their old age, but not Maud. Gardens were good, but she had better things to do.

Maud owned and operated a number of businesses. In her spare time she traveled the world. She actually liked to hunt because her Daddy taught her how. It was funny, seeing an old woman in her nineties hunt, but Maud pulled it off like a pro. She would often leave the office on a split-decision. "Lunch at Faster Burger?" she might think. "No way, how about kangaroo from the outback, or rhino roast from Africa." Then she'd leave the office, jump in her own airplane and fly there. She'd go to Africa and hunt down the ferocious rhino for lunch. Then maybe she'd pick off a lion or two just to have them stuffed and mounted at one of her offices! She didn't care if it was illegal. Those kind of laws were intended for other people. Not experienced hunters like herself.

Today, Maud was better known as Mean Maud. The nickname came with her old age. It wasn't because she liked to hunt either. It was because her skin had grown so wrinkled that she looked like she had a permanent frown on her face. She looked mean, even though she was actually a nice woman.

The nickname, Mean Maud, carried over to most of her businesses. She had several large car dealerships, and they were all known as Mean Maud's Motors. Normally people wouldn't buy a car from a woman named Mean Maud, but

Maud's commercials made it look like a good thing. They even used her unusual hunting nature. The television and radio commercials portrayed Maud as a hateful, gun-carrying hillbilly on the hunt for a good car deal. She would hold car salesmen at gunpoint while customers happily drove away with their good deal. The Mean Maud character worked well in commercials. Customers loved it, and they flocked to Mean Maud's Motors to get their good deal on a car.

Maud's business was mostly honest. She sold her cars at a fair price, and they were always good vehicles. But secretly, Maud sometimes bought her cars from bad places. That's how Seth Slaughter knew her. Maud couldn't pass on a good car deal, even if it was on the black market from some criminal.

Cars from criminals were usually stolen. The thief would break into somebody's car and steal it. Then they'd slap on a new paint job to make it look different. The cars were often really nice too. Criminals would trick them out with stolen stereos, tinted windows, lift kits and fancy wheels.

Criminals would deliver these super-nice cars to Maud and she bought them every time, because the criminals sold them so cheap. That meant that Maud could resell them at an honest price, but still make more money than usual. It was a win for the criminals, a win for the car buyers and a really profitable win for Maud.

This part of the business wasn't honest. Maud knew that. She was secretly helping underground low-lifes. But Maud told herself that it was okay to do it. After all, somebody had to purchase the stolen cars and get a great deal. Why shouldn't it be her?

Everything else Maud did was legit. She was honest with her car sales, and the customers continued to come in for their great deal from Mean Maud. She was a little famous because of the good deals and the commercials.

Cars weren't the only things Maud sold. She also had a few boat dealerships on Lake Champlain in Vermont. Her 'Mean Maud' promotions carried over to the boats too. Commercials showed her chasing salesmen onto a sinking boat if they wouldn't give her the deal she wanted.

Maud also took over a small business near the United States border, between Vermont and Canada. It was kind of a family heirloom. She lovingly called it her father's place, because it reminded her of her Daddy and their times together when she was a kid. Nothing was sold here. Instead, people could pay to come in and look at interesting things from the past, like a museum.

Maud usually put her hunting trophies on display here, she had to put them somewhere. The stuffed lions, rhinoceroses and other exotic creatures were unusual and interesting, so they fit in perfectly with the other displays. Maud had thought about adding an exotic cafe to the museum. She could sell rhino roast and kangaroo steaks. That way she wouldn't have to fly to Africa or Australia for an exotic lunch. But that would also take the fun out of the hunting she loved so much, so she never added the cafe.

The museum didn't make any money. In fact, Maud lost money trying to keep it open. She didn't mind, though. She made so much money with cars and boats that this didn't bother her.

Maud hated sitting in her office on days like today. It was beautiful and sunny. She usually didn't go to work on days like this, but today was different. There was a problem.

Some escaped criminal had posted a couple of videos on Facetube, updating his travel progress after escaping the prison. During the last video, he spoke directly to Maud. The fool actually said, "Maud, you're in this area. If you see this video, I need you to find me a boat."

"Idiot," Maud said to herself. "He's practically telling the police that he wants a boat from me! He's almost telling them that I'm a criminal and then he dares the police to find him! Good grief."

Seth's video, calling out to Maud, got a lot of attention from the local news media. News anchors spoke about Maud during their live broadcasts.

"Who is Maud?" they asked each other. "Could this be Mean Maud from Mean Maud's Boats? If so, how does Seth know Mean Maud? Has he purchased boats from her in the past?"

It was all foolish talk. Nobody could prove that Mean Maud was whom Seth Slaughter spoke about. It was an interesting thought though, so it became the subject of a lot of local gossip.

Maud studied the Facetube video. She listened to what Seth had to say, but she also considered the part of the video with Edwin Slaughter. Then there was the live video of the lake monster named Champ. She showed no expression while watching the video, only the mean look that her face usually portrayed.

Maud watched the video several times. She finally

seemed satisfied and stopped. She turned her office chair towards the window and stared outside. "I could really use some rhino roast about now," Maud said to herself. "A nice break, away from society. Maybe the outback is what I need." Then, turning back to the computer, she added, "That Seth is such a dummy! I have no idea how that kid got so much accomplished before going to jail. He's so stupid!"

Maud turned to look at an old picture sitting at the corner of her desk. It was black and white and it portrayed a young Maud with a grizzly looking man in a beard. It was her father, and the two of them looked very happy. Maud picked up the picture and spoke to it.

"What would you do Daddy? I know, I know. Family comes first, but how do I deliver a boat without getting into trouble? Especially if it's fully loaded! And if I get away with it, what do I do about Edwin? He's no drunk Daddy, but he's as obsessed as you were. There's no stopping him. What would you do?"

Maud turned and looked out the window again. "Maybe," she said to herself. "Maybe I can help Edwin. You know, help him get what he wants. That way I can rein him in a bit and calm him down. But how? What could I do?"

A smile stretched across her wrinkled face as an idea began to form in her head. "That's an interesting thought," she said. "What if we made a business out of it?"

CHAPTER 15
DRAKES EAT FISH DINNER

That evening the Drake family gathered around the campfire and enjoyed a delicious fish dinner. Uncle Jim was the champ at cooking fish on a fire. He grilled it with a special concoction of spices and seasonings. Then he loaded a mixture of grilled onions, peppers and tomatoes on top. The kids would normally run from vegetables like that at home, but somehow they liked Uncle Jim's recipe.

Following dinner, the kids took a phone call from their Mom. She just checked in, to see how everything had gone. Norah was more excited than the boys to talk with her. "I miss you Mommy," she repeated four or five times. The boys each took a chance to say "Hi," and then the call was over.

After that, Jim surprised the kids with a special treat. A blackberry cobbler, cooked inside a Dutch oven. Plus he made homemade ice cream to go on top! Everyone loved it.

The boys stuffed themselves silly. Norah ate quite a bit too. There was still food on her plate when she turned away and walked over to Uncle Jim. She climbed onto his lap and turned to watch the campfire. She was now almost asleep. Her little head was bobbing up and down. Her eyes would slowly close and then her head would fall. She'd pick it back up and stare at the fire for a moment and then the process would repeat. Uncle Jim leaned back in his chair and laid her head on his chest. She fought it at first, but then gave in.

The night was growing cold so the warmth from the fire felt good. It was the perfect time to visit the lake and camp out. It would get cold tonight, but everyone would be comfy when they snuggled up inside their thick sleeping bags.

Noah thought the stars at Lake Champlain seemed brighter than the ones at home. Then again, maybe he didn't get out enough to enjoy the ones at home. This was about the only time he ever camped out.

The day had been a good one. There were no sightings of Champ, but there had been a lot of fish. Plus Noah had caught the huge sturgeon. Uncle Jim lost it, but that was okay. Nobody had caught anything bigger anyway. Noah smiled to himself.

"I guess I won the fishing competition today," he said out loud. "Nobody got anything as large as my sturgeon."

"What sturgeon?" asked Nathan. "I don't see any sturgeon."

"You know what sturgeon I'm talking about," said Noah. "It was only the biggest fish any of us have ever caught. It was bigger than you!"

"I don't see it," said Nathan. He poked a stick into the fire and played with the embers. "I don't know what you're talking about."

Noah took a deep breath and stared at the fire.

The boys had started to argue after the fishing trip. They got along before then, but somehow the peace was over. Maybe it was too late in the day to get along. Maybe the boys needed some time away from each other. Maybe they just needed to suck it up and get along.

"Everyone knows I caught the biggest fish of the day," said Noah.

"I don't know it," said Nathan.

"Yes you do!" said Noah in anger. "You're the one that said we'd have to keep it, even if it was endangered."

"Well," said Nathan. "I may have said that, but the truth is that I brought home the largest catch of the day. We all ate it for dinner."

Noah rolled his eyes in aggravation and said, "Whatever Nathan."

Nathan repeated his brother in a mocking tone, "Whatever Noah."

"That's enough you two," said Uncle Jim. "Can't you guys get along?"

Norah's eyes popped open for a brief moment and then they gently shut as she rested on Uncle Jim's chest.

"Uncle Jim?" asked Noah. "What was that you said about Champ chasing the sturgeon?"

Uncle Jim laughed. "Last month I spotted one of the babies chasing after a sturgeon. I'm sure it was trying to catch the sturgeon to eat. I just thought it was kind of funny, given the legend of Captain Crum."

"Captain Crunch?" asked Nathan with a smile.

"No," said Uncle Jim. "Captain Crum. You remember him Noah, right? Last summer you told us how you read about his encounter with Champ in the 1800s."

Noah looked to the side and thought for a moment. "Was that the guy who saw Champ from a distance and guessed she was really long, and had a star on her head?" asked Noah.

"Yeah," said Uncle Jim. "In 1819 Captain Crum said he saw Champ. He estimated the lake monster was almost 200 feet long. A far cry from what I've seen. I can't even imagine one that size. Anyway, his story says a few fish were chasing Champ and two of them were sturgeon."

"That's right," said Noah. "I remember that." He smiled. "And now Champ's chasing the sturgeon."

"Yeah," said Uncle Jim. "I thought that was kind of funny."

"So how much do you really see Champ?" asked Nathan.

"Oh, not too often," said Uncle Jim. "I've seen her babies a little more, but I probably get a glimpse of something every few months."

"I'm hoping we get to see her again," said Noah. "I want to get a good picture that we can show Dad. He might believe in Champ if we get a good enough picture."

"Your dad still doesn't believe in Champ?" asked Uncle Jim.

"No way," said Nathan. "It's like he refuses to believe."

"I hate to tell you guys," said Uncle Jim, "but a picture may not help your situation."

"Why not?" asked Noah.

"Like Nathan said, it's like your dad doesn't want to believe," said Uncle Jim. "Plus a good picture may not be enough. Usually lake monsters keep their head in the water. When people see them, they usually don't know what they are. It's just some unknown object moving through the water. A lake monster usually looks like a log or an upside down boat. It's Champ's body, but people don't realize that. And a picture, a flat piece of photo paper, doesn't give a good representation of what you really see."

"So we need a picture of Champ out of the water?" asked Noah.

"That would be very good," said Uncle Jim. "But that's not always perfect either. Sandra Mansi got a great picture of Champ in the nineteen-seventies, head and all. People still didn't believe her though."

"Sandra Mansi?" asked Noah.

"Yeah," said Uncle Jim. "Look up the Sandra Mansi photo on the internet. There's tons of stuff about it. But I bet your Dad still wouldn't believe in Champ, even if he saw that."

"Why not?" asked Nathan.

Uncle Jim took a deep breath. "Well," he said, "maybe he's just been taught too much evolution and public school science. Sometimes it takes a lot to change a person's point of view. It did me. I've heard stories of Champ for years! But I didn't believe any of them until she knocked me out of my boat!"

"True," said Nathan.

"But you believe now," said Noah.

"Yeah," said Uncle Jim. "But I didn't back then. Before I met Champ, I thought lake monster believers were silly. I don't know. Maybe I thought they were push-overs, like they'd believe in anything. I didn't want to be that way. I didn't want to have the wool pulled over my eyes."

"But it was," said Nathan.

"No," said Noah. "He already had the wool pulled over his eyes. He didn't want to believe what was right in front of him."

"That's true," said Uncle Jim. "Not until it knocked me out of my boat. That encounter pulled my head out of the hole and made a believer out of me!"

"So that's what Dad needs?" asked Noah.

"Maybe so," said Uncle Jim. "But it's hard to create that kind of circumstance. Until then, just keep preaching to the choir. Keep telling him about Champ. Keep showing your evidence. You might win him over. If you don't, at least you'll educate him."

"That's like trying to tell people about Jesus," said Nathan. "They may not believe anything you say, but you just keep telling them what you know. One day you might say the right thing. You might answer the one question that they couldn't figure out. And if you don't, it's no biggie. At least you're filling their head with good information that somebody else might be able to help them sift through!"

"That's right," said Uncle Jim. "That's a lot like what Paul said to the Corinthians in the Bible. He was talking about training baby Christians."

"Baby Christians?" asked Nathan.

"Yeah," said Uncle Jim. "Paul said a new Christian, being born into the Kingdom of God, is like a baby. When Norah was a baby, did your dad ever grill a steak on the grill and feed it to her?"

"No," laughed Nathan. "She couldn't eat steak! She'd throw it on the ground."

"That's right," said Uncle Jim. "Baby Christians are just like that. You can't give them something complicated to chew on. You have to feed them the milk of the Word. The simpler things, like the Ten Commandments or the story of Jesus."

"I never thought about that," said Nathan.

"Steak is delicious, and it's good for the body," said Uncle Jim. "But a baby doesn't have teeth. They can't bite into it. So you keep feeding it milk. One day that baby will grow up, get teeth and be able to bite into tougher foods. Baby Christians grow in the Word and bite into tougher subjects. They get closer to God and develop a relationship with Him."

"So you're saying, if we keep telling Dad what we know about Champ and lake monsters, that one day he might believe us?" asked Noah.

"Yes," said Uncle Jim. "Keep feeding him the knowledge you have. Keep pouring in that milk. One day, God willing, he'll be able to eat some steak."

CHAPTER 16
THE BAIT WORKS

Seth Slaughter was lying in his tent, alone in the campground. He was impressed with himself. Things were really coming together and it felt like he was finally becoming the famous criminal he always wanted to be. He had escaped from prison and the police hadn't found him! His Facetube account was littered with hits from video watchers that seemed to love him. Mean Maud had even brought him a ritzy, high dollar yacht.

Seth couldn't understand how Maud could find him, yet the police couldn't. In the end, he figured she must have more power. Either way, Seth was enjoying her luxurious gift. The boat had plenty of power and it was fully stocked with the extras he had hoped for. It even had a couple rooms below the deck! Life couldn't get any better!

Then there was Seth's foot. It had grown so sore that Seth couldn't stand it. Even with everything going so well, life seemed unbearable because of the pain in his toe.

Seth's toe didn't stop Grandpa Edwin though. Edwin was ecstatic about the hunt for Champ. He had a boat, the Slaughter Hook, his special bait and even a motorized winch to reel in the lake monster. This was about as good as it could get for Edwin.

Edwin wanted Seth's help, of course. He even pleaded with Seth to go with him to catch Champ, but Seth refused. His foot hurt so bad that he wouldn't get up. He wouldn't leave the camp. He wouldn't do anything. Instead, he stayed in his sleeping bag in hopes he could "sleep off" the pain. Edwin finally gave up and left without him. He was gone before dawn.

When Seth finally woke up, he turned over and grabbed his smartphone. He downloaded some video games and spent some time playing. At first it was fun. He'd get the hang of the game and how it played. But then he'd have to quit because the game wanted money to go to the next level. He downloaded and tried several games, but they all ended the same way. Finally, in frustration, he stopped playing.

Instead, he browsed through his Facetube videos to see if there were any new likes or comments. There were quite a few, actually. Most of them had something to do with Seth's escape or with Seth's sighting of Champ.

"Way to go Seth!" said one comment. "Show those

coppers who's the boss! Be sure to keep us posted on your progress!"

"You're a criminal!" said another. "I hope the police catch you soon and put you back behind bars where you belong."

"Champ - Shamp," said a third. "There's no Champ, you're full of beans! I've seen better effects at a high school musical!"

"Seriously," Seth said to himself. "People can't believe something right in front of their eyes! Now I know what Grandpa, and even Great Grandpa, felt like! Even when people see the proof, they still can't accept it!"

The last comment was supportive. "Way to go Seth! I've been trying to get a video of Champ for years! Can't believe you got him on your first try! You're one lucky guy! If your luck keeps going, those coppers will never catch you!"

"That's right," Seth said to himself. "Those Coppers ain't got a chance!"

Seth was satisfied. He didn't care that a few haters didn't like him, that was no big deal. Seth was used to haters with his line of work. Nobody likes you when you're the boss, especially when you're the criminal boss.

Seth decided to broadcast another live video. He tapped a button and pointed the camera at his face.

"Hello Facetubers! Seth Slaughter here, on the shores of," he paused a moment so he could think of what to say. "On the shores of some, uh, unknown water front here." He waved his hands and gestured to the unknown water. "Right here in the middle of the country! That's right, some unknown area, somewhere in the world." He stared at the camera like a deer caught in a pair of headlights. "Oh who am I kidding? I'm still on Lake Champlain with Grandpa Slaughter. It's no matter, you won't find me."

"Things are pretty dull right now. I'm enjoying a little rest while my Grandpa tries to catch Champ, the lake monster."

He leaned towards the camera. "There really is a lake monster, you know? If you don't believe me, watch that last video. I have proof that Champ is right here, in Lake Champlain!"

"Now, you're probably thinking to yourself," he leaned back and spoke in a different voice. "Hey Seth, what's next? You just got out of jail, you're on the run from the police, and now you've witnessed a living dinosaur in the middle of a lake! What are you going to do now?"

"I'll tell you what I'm going to do," said Seth. "Nothing!" He laughed. "I'm going to sit right here and relax at this campground. Let my grandfather do all the work! He's the one with the plan to catch Champ, let him do it! But what if Grandpa's plan doesn't work? What if things don't happen the way he plans? Well, let's just say I've got an idea that will make everything work out. I'm saying, this whole mess will be cleaned up." He leaned toward the camera and said, "Wink, wink! I've got some good connections, you know what I mean?"

Seth leaned back in his seat and continued talking to the camera. "I'll tell you what though, Grandpa's no fool. He's got a plan of Biblical proportion, literally! No seriously, he took his plan directly from the pages of the Bible. It's literally a plan of Biblical proportion!"

"However, it stinks! I mean the bait stinks, not the plan. That's part of the reason why I'm sitting here at camp. I don't care to be around that stinky stuff. So let's let Grandpa do it himself! I'll just sit here and relax."

Seth unwrapped a candy sucker and stuck it in his mouth. He rolled it from cheek to cheek, seeming to really enjoy it. Then he popped the sucker out and said, "Grandpa's out fishing, right now. He's got the hook baited and he's hoping Champ will take a bite and get snagged. I'm sure the monster will take it. He seemed to like the smell when Gramps was cooking!"

Seth set the camera down, pointing it at his face. He thought for a minute, rolling the sucker from cheek to cheek. In the distance, behind Seth, Grandpa Edwin walked into the camera's view. He looked like he was dragging something large and heavy. He stopped for a moment to drop what he was dragging. Then he placed his hands on his hips and arched his back. A moment later he picked up the heavy thing and began dragging it again. It looked like hard work, but he slowly grew closer.

Seth didn't notice, but he did look like he had something to say. He picked up the camera and began to talk. "You know, while I was in the slammer I had some time to think. Well, actually I had a lot of time to think. You see, I was in jail because a couple of knuckle-heads decided I didn't need to be in charge of my own business. They tried to push me out so they could take over my, uh, profession. So I hurt them."

Seth's face changed as he looked into the camera. It took on a look of hate, as if Seth would never forgive the guys that had done him wrong. "If you guys are watching now, I want to tell you something. He leaned towards the camera, took out his sucker and used it to point at the screen. "Jethro, Sully, be forewarned! I hurt you once, but I don't think I'm done. If I ever see you again, I'm gonna..." Seth stopped talking. He suddenly heard footsteps in the background.

"Somebody's here!" he said. He turned the camera around and noticed Edwin. "It's Grandpa! And he's got something! Could it be? No way. But yes, it looks like he caught Champ! It's impossible! Was it really that easy?!"

Seth tried to jump in his excitement. It didn't work. His body stood alright, but then he was back on the ground. "Stupid toe," he muttered to himself. But he didn't let it stop him. Instead, he got up again and hobbled towards his grandfather. The camera jostled up and down, back and forth. The sound of Seth's feet, half dragging through the brush, could be heard behind the noise of the camera handling.

"Did you get it Grandpa?" he asked breathlessly. "Did you catch Champ? Did you really do it?!"

Grandpa stopped and stretched his back again. "No ya dummy," said Grandpa Edwin. "And would you put that stupid thing away?"

"Not yet Gramps," said Seth. He pointed the camera at his face and said, "I want to see what you caught! I want to show everybody what my Grandpa caught!"

"I caught dinner," said Grandpa Edwin. "That's all I got."

"Dinner?" asked Seth, totally disappointed. "I thought

you were working! I thought you were trying to catch Champ!"

"I was trying to catch Champ, you fool!" said Grandpa Edwin. He was still leaning back in order to stretch out his back. "But all I got was this stupid sturgeon."

The fish lying at Grandpa Edwin's feet was the largest one Seth had ever seen in the wild.

"Did you say that's a sturgeon?" asked Seth. "Why'd you catch it?"

"Because I thought it was Champ!" said Grandpa Edwin. "The fish fooled me! It kept stealing the bait off my hook, I had to use it all! Then, when I finally caught him, he died!"

"Well, that must mean the bait works," said Seth.

"Yeah, but now we'll need more if we want to catch Champ," said Grandpa Edwin. He let out a sigh. "At least we still have some extra ingredients."

"Well, this really stinks," said Seth. Then he laughed when he realized what he said. "I mean the fish stinks because of the bait, but this situation stinks because we didn't catch Champ."

Grandpa Edwin rolled his eyes. "At least we'll have a good dinner tonight, and maybe tomorrow night, and the night after that, and the night after that. That's if we can keep it all fresh, of course. It's the largest sturgeon I've ever seen. It must be seven feet long!"

Edwin found a chair in the middle of the camp and eased himself into it. "The big stinker fooled me! I thought I'd caught Champ for sure. It even put up a fight when I reeled him in, though it didn't last long. It was already dead by the time I pulled it up, onto the boat. I guess the bait worked fast. Then again, he had already eaten his fair share before I caught him."

"Then that means the bait works!" said Seth. "The fish like it and they die when they eat it!"

"Of course it works, ya dummy," said Grandpa Edwin. "What else would you expect it to do?"

"Maybe I should feed some to you," said Seth. "Ya old coot."

"What'd you say?" asked Grandpa Edwin.

"Uh," stuttered Seth. "Nothing, it was nothing."

"I'm telling you," said Grandpa Edwin, "I thought I had Champ. I felt like your great grandpap Sammy was right there with me, saying 'Good job boy.' But then it was this stupid fish."

Seth stopped listening. Instead, he turned the camera back toward his face. "Oh well. I guess it's been a disappointing day," he said. "But my Gramps isn't done yet. He still has to do a lot of work so we can catch this lake monster! So you just sit back and relax, I know I will. Then we'll get some more video and have something amazing to show you. Just stay tuned! Before I finish this video I want to tell you one more thing." Seth held the camera up high and pointed it at his face. "You'll never catch me coppers! Over and out!"

CHAPTER 17
SOMETHING SMELLS FISHY

Early the next morning Noah, Nathan, Norah and Uncle Jim were up and hiking the trail through the woods. They had already passed The Old Gentleman, the tree that bends low, and continued straight on the trail. They weren't going to fish today, they were going to rent a boat and go tubing.

Little Norah had already been crying because she couldn't walk any further. Nathan offered to help, but Uncle Jim decided he'd carry her on his shoulders. This made her real happy.

"I can grab the leaves!" she said, grabbing a tree limb.

"Yeah," said Uncle Jim. "But you can't hold them.

They'll pull you off my shoulders!" He stopped and waited for her to let go.

"Awww," she whined. "Okay Unca' Jim."

Norah let go of the limb and it whipped backwards behind her. Noah saw it coming, but Nathan didn't. It slapped him in the face and knocked him to the ground. Noah laughed.

"Stop laughing," said Nathan. "It's not funny!"

"Yeah, it is!" said Noah. "You should have seen your face! Your eyes were as big as a DVD!"

Uncle Jim turned around just in time. Nathan grabbed a rock and threw it at Noah. He missed of course, but Uncle Jim saw the attack.

"That's enough!" said Uncle Jim. "I know it's early, but you two need to stop fighting! We're on vacation, we're going tubing."

"Not with reflexes like Nathan's," said Noah. "He's just gonna fall in and go swimming."

Nathan grabbed another rock.

"Put that down," said Uncle Jim firmly. "And Noah, stop insulting your brother."

"It's not an insult," said Noah. "It's the truth!"

"It is an insult," said Uncle Jim. "And I'm tired of you doing it to Nathan!" He looked at Nathan and held out his hand to help him up.

"And so am I," said Nathan.

Noah took a deep breath, turned and began to walk the trail. Behind him he could hear Nathan and Uncle Jim talk.

"He needs to take a chill-pill," said Nathan.

"That's enough," said Uncle Jim. "Let it go and let's

enjoy the morning."

"Okay," said Nathan. "I'm sorry Uncle Jim."

"It's alright," said Uncle Jim. "I remember what it's like being a brother. Your father and I used to fight all the time. We'd give anything to help each other out, but we still fought."

Noah tried to ignore the two talking, but he couldn't help listening. His brother was so infuriating. He was clumsy too! It wasn't Noah's fault that he looked funny when the tree limb smacked him in the face. Noah smiled at the thought.

Noah continued walking the trail, but slowed down. A new scent was in the air and it was horrible smelling. It was like a mixture of highway road and burnt fish. It wasn't like anything he had smelled before. He turned towards the foul odor. It was down the hill on the left.

"What's up?" asked Uncle Jim. Then he froze, smelling the stench in the air.

"Do you have gas Noah?" asked Norah. "You stink." She waved at the air in an effort to push the smell away.

"It's not me Norah," said Noah.

"Somebody's burning something," said Uncle Jim. "It's something awful too."

The Drake family looked through the brush, trying to figure out where the smell was coming from.

"Do you guys mind if we stop and have a look?" asked Uncle Jim. "I want to make sure everything is alright."

"Sure!" said Nathan.

"Yeah," said Noah. "I'm curious too."

"Awww Unca' Jim," whined Norah. "I want to go

tubing."

"We will Norah," said Uncle Jim. "But let's see what's going on first."

Uncle Jim put Norah down and held her hand. He led her, and the boys, down the hill. The smell grew stronger.

"What is that?" asked Nathan. "It's horrible!"

"Noah, you really stink!" said Norah.

"It's not me," said Noah. "It's Nathan."

Uncle Jim turned and looked at Noah and Nathan just in time to see Nathan punch Noah in the chest. Jim stared at the two boys. They both looked at the ground. He turned around and continued towards the smell.

In a few moments they overheard an argument.

"I don't care if your foot hurts," said one voice. "All you've done is sit around and play on that stupid phone. Get off your butt and help me take this food to the boat! It'll ruin if we don't get it to a refrigerator."

"No," said another voice. "Somebody has to stay with the bait. To make sure it doesn't burn."

"I think it's too late for that," whispered Nathan.

"It's tar and fish guts," said the first voice. "It's not going to burn."

"But what about the hair?" asked the second voice.

"We can mix it in when we get back," said the first voice.

"No," said the second. "I'm staying here."

Uncle Jim turned and looked at the two boys. "They sound about as bad as you two," he teased. Noah and Nathan both rolled their eyes.

The Drakes could see where the smell was coming from now. There was a clearing ahead that overlooked the lake.

On this side of the clearing was a tent, a canopy and a black pot sitting on a campfire. The pot was spewing out an ugly, thick and black smoke.

"That must be where the smell's coming from," said Nathan.

"You think?" asked Noah.

"Shush," said Uncle Jim.

"Yeah, shush," said Norah.

The Drakes stopped walking and stood behind a bush, overlooking the campsite. Any further and they'd be in the clearing.

"Fine ya big dummy," said the voice they first heard. "Fine. You sit here and play on your stupid phone. I need a break from you anyway. I thought you were here to help, but I guess not."

The man turned around and walked towards the waterfront.

"That guy looks familiar," said Nathan.

"I'm not sure I like this," said Uncle Jim. "I'm going to call the police."

"He sounds familiar too," said Nathan.

"Which one?" asked Noah. "The one that stormed off or the one that's sitting around?"

"The one that stormed off," said Nathan.

"Yeah," said Noah. "I think that's me in the future. You're the one that sits on his butt all day. See, that guy gets tired of it too. It's tough when family sits around on their butt all day."

Noah didn't see it coming. The wind knocked out of his lungs as Nathan tackled him. He was knocked to the ground and Nathan started punching his belly.

"Get off me!" wheezed Noah.

"No!" shouted Nathan. "You take it back! You stop insulting me!"

"Stop fighting," screamed Norah. "Stop fighting!"

Uncle Jim dropped his phone to grab Nathan and Noah. He pulled both boys to their feet, holding them equally at arms length. "I've had it," he said. "All you two have done is fight, fight, fight. We're headed back to camp and you can both sit around like the lazy guy over there."

"But I wanna go tubing!" said Norah.

"I'm sorry Norah," said Uncle Jim. "But we're not going to go tubing today. Your brothers ruined it for everybody."

"I'll say they did," said a new voice. It was Seth Slaughter. He stood a few feet away with his rifle pointed at Uncle Jim.

"Who, who are you?" asked Uncle Jim. "What are you doing?"

"Oh, don't you know?" asked Seth. "I'm the lazy guy that you were just talking about. You know, the one that sits around all day?"

CHAPTER 18
CAUGHT!

"Put that gun down!" said Uncle Jim. "You have no right to point it at us."

Jim Drake held out his arms, guarding Noah, Nathan and Norah behind him. He was ready to take a bullet for his brother's kids, but he would be sure to take down the man with the gun if it happened.

"No," said Seth Slaughter. "I think I have every right to hold you at gunpoint. You've been spying on me!"

"We weren't spying," said Uncle Jim. "We were just trying to see what the horrible smell was!"

"It is pretty bad, isn't it?" asked Seth. "But I still think you're spying. You said, and I quote, 'You two can both sit around like the lazy guy over there.' That means you overheard me and Gramps arguing, and that means I should keep you for a little while. We don't need any more trouble at this point."

"What?!" asked Uncle Jim. "So what if we heard you two have an argument? What's so bad about that?"

"Well, I don't know what all you heard," said Seth. "I can't have you leave and report me to the cops now, can I?"

"The cops?!" asked Nathan.

"That's what he said," muttered Noah.

"Be quiet," Uncle Jim spat at the two boys.

Seth pointed the rifle at the family with renewed vigor.

Uncle Jim cleared his throat and said, "Excuse me sir. Why would we call the cops over you burning, what was it? Tar and fish guts?"

"Ahh, so you did hear what we were talking about," said Seth.

"Wait a sec," said Nathan. "I know who you are."

"You do?" asked Seth. "Have you been watching Facetube?"

"Huh?" asked Nathan.

"I just thought that maybe you were a subscriber to my channel," said Seth.

"Um, no," said Nathan. "But I met your brother Frankie. You look, and sound, a lot like him. You must be Seth Slaughter!"

"Shoot," said Seth. "I thought maybe I had some loyal fans here for an autograph."

"Wow," said Noah. "Nathan's right! You're the spitting

image of Frankie. Well, except for the hair."

"Yeah," said Nathan. "Frankie has some."

"Hey now," said Seth. "I have hair, just not a lot. They cut it real short when you're in prison."

"Oh stop," said Nathan. "We're not dumb. We can see you're bald."

"Wow," said Seth, sliding a hand over his bald head. "Did your momma teach you those good manners?" Then he said to Uncle Jim, "I see why you were yelling at them."

"You have no idea," said Uncle Jim.

The two boys looked at Uncle Jim and raised their eyebrows.

"It's not my fault," said Jim. "You two were fighting."

Noah looked at Seth and said, "So was that Grandpa Edwin that just left?"

"Yeah," said Seth. "The old goat's mad at me."

"Why do you sit on your butt all day?" asked Norah.

Seth looked at her with interest. "It's because of my foot, little girl," he said. "I got shot in my foot. It hurts."

Norah eyed him with suspicion. "Well don't shoot my foot," she said. "I don't want it to hurt like yours."

Seth smiled at her. "You have spunk!" he said. "I like you."

"I'm not a skunk!" said Norah. She pointed at Noah and said, "Noah's the skunk. He has gas."

Noah rolled his eyes. "I told you Norah, it's not me! It's that stinky pot of tar and fish they're cooking over there."

"That's right," said Seth, lifting the rifle back up towards Noah. "It's tar and fish. And yes," he looked towards Norah. "It smells horrible, but it does work!"

"Work? What does it do?" asked Nathan.

"Come to the camp and I'll tell you all about it," said Seth.

"Um," said Uncle Jim. "Thanks, but we'd rather not. I think we'll just head back to our camp." He turned like he was ready to leave.

"You don't have a choice," said Seth. He cocked the gun for emphasis. "Besides, you want to know what I'm cooking, don't you?"

From on the ground, Uncle Jim's phone began to ring. Seth picked it up and read who was calling.

"Marie Drake," he said. "Is that anyone important?"

"Mommy!" said Norah.

"Well, in that case I'd better hang onto this," said Seth and he pocketed the phone. "Come on. Let's go see what's cooking. You first."

Uncle Jim looked at the three kids. "How do we get into these messes?" he said.

Norah pointed at Noah and Nathan. "It's their fault Unca' Jim."

Jim rolled his eyes and said "You know Norah, your mom is going to kill me."

"No Unca' Jim," she said. "I won't let her."

Jim grabbed Norah's hand and said "Come on let's do what the man with the gun says."

He led Norah and the boys towards Seth's camp, and the smelly pot on the fire. Seth followed the family. When they got near the fire he pointed to a patch of dirt and said, "Pop a squat." Then he loped to a folding chair and sat down, placing the rifle on his lap.

"So what's the smelly stuff for?" asked Noah.

"It's bait," said Seth. "It's an old recipe Gramps is using to catch and kill a lake monster."

"You're trying to kill Champ again?" asked Noah.

"Seriously?" asked Nathan.

"Yeah," said Seth.

"And you think this stinky stuff will work?" asked Noah.

"I know it will," said Seth. "We've already tested it. Champ came to us the first time we made a batch. Well, one of the babies did."

"Did you kill it?" asked Nathan.

"No," said Seth. "The bait wasn't ready. But I did get it on video!"

"Really?" asked Nathan. "Can I see?"

"Yeah," Seth said proudly. "Just check out my Facetube channel. I'm getting tons of likes."

"Cool!" said Nathan.

"But, how does the bait kill Champ?" asked Noah.

"Well, you see that trash bag full of hair between you and the fire?" asked Seth.

"Yeah," said Noah.

"We mix it in the bait," said Seth. "It makes a gigantic hair ball that we can use as bait to catch Champ. He likes this smell because of the fish guts, so he'll try to eat it. But he can't digest it because of the hair and tar."

"Oh wow," said Nathan. "That sounds like what the prophet Daniel did in those two extra books in the Catholic Bible."

"It is," said Seth. "That's where the idea came from! Apparently my great grandfather, Sea-Monster Sammy,

147

figured it out ages ago."

"But how do you know it will work?" asked Noah.

"You smell those fish guts?" asked Seth. "That's part of a huge Lake Sturgeon that Gramps caught. It ate the last batch of bait that we made. I'd say the bait works well because the sturgeon ate all of it."

"Oh wow," said Nathan.

"Yeah," said Seth. "Gramps was pretty upset about losing all the bait. But the sturgeon died quickly. In fact, it was gone by the time Gramps reeled it in." Seth bent over and grabbed a magazine from off the ground. He flipped through the pages.

Noah's mind began to churn. He remembered the recipe and reviewed it out loud. "So the fish guts attract Champ, the hair makes the bait inedible and the tar keeps it all together." He asked Seth, "Is that how it works?"

"I don't know how it all works buddy," said Seth. He didn't even look up from his magazine. "I just know that it does work."

"It's such a simple recipe," said Noah. "That must be how it works."

"Noah?" asked Nathan.

But Noah ignored him. He was trying to figure out how they could save Champ. If the bait killed the sturgeon that quickly, it could do the same for Champ. There had to be something they could do to mess up Grandpa Edwin's plan again.

CHAPTER 19
NO CONTACT

"I'm telling you Marie," said John Drake. "Christian Star was the highlight of the convention!"

"I know, I know," said Marie. "You can't stop talking about him. I even went to sleep, and when I woke up, you kept going!"

It was true. Marie and John had been on the road for several hours, and John told Marie all about Christian Star. Even after a two-hour nap, Marie woke up and John spoke some more.

"Well honey, you don't get to meet a guy like that everyday. Think about it, he's in all our favorite movies:

Burnproof, Right Up Front, and even that cool documentary called Losing Easter."

"And who can forget," teased Marie. "His old classic TV show Shrinking Pains!"

"No, no. That's Shrinking Relief!" said John.

"Oops," said Marie, grinning. "I forgot, it was before my time."

"Not mine," said John. "And I got to meet him!"

"Isn't it wonderful?" said Marie, rolling her eyes.

"Yes it is," said John.

Marie stared at her husband. She loved him, but she was concerned that he hadn't gotten anything of value from the conference.

"John?" asked Marie. "Did you learn anything about being a homeschool Dad?"

"What?" asked John, still star struck.

"We went to a homeschool convention," said Marie. "One of the biggest in the country. Did you learn anything about being a homeschool dad? Or did you just walk away with Christian Star's autograph?"

"Of course I got his autograph," said John.

Marie frowned, but continued to stare at her husband. It took a minute, but he finally noticed. He did a double take when he realized she was frowning.

"Marie, I learned a lot," said John. "Christian was full of information."

"Really?" asked Marie. "Like what?"

"Like how important it is to support my wife," said John. "You do a lot Marie! Actually, you do everything."

"Oh really?" she asked.

"Yes!" said John. "Christian pointed out how our wives are often the brains behind the whole operation."

"Is that so?" Marie smiled. She knew John was fishing for what to say.

"Yes!" said John. "You do all the heavy lifting. All I do is make the money so you can stay home and do it! And actually, I can't understand how you stay with all three kids, all day long every day. All they do is pull at you and ask for more!"

Marie patted John's leg. "It's not that bad," she said. "I love our kids!"

"Well I do too," said John. "But I can't do what you do. I'm just glad we got to take a break and get away, just the two of us. It was real nice."

"Yes it was," agreed Marie. "It was good to get a break."

"Maybe we should extend it," said John. "We could stop over in Buffalo and enjoy another night."

"Oh John," said Marie. "That would be nice, but I miss our kids. We need to make sure they're not driving your brother nuts. Speaking of which, I'm going to try calling them again."

Marie had tried calling before they left, but Uncle Jim didn't answer. Marie wasn't too worried, they were on vacation after all. She just wanted to make sure everything was all right.

"I'm sure they're fine," said John.

Marie dialed the number to call Uncle Jim's phone. It rang on the other end of the line, but Uncle Jim never answered. The call just went to voicemail. Marie tried again, just in case Jim didn't get to the phone in time. It rang and rang, then went to voicemail again. She tried one more time, just to make sure. Nobody answered. She put her phone down and looked out the window. She missed her kids.

"I don't understand why he won't answer," said Marie.

"Well, maybe he's out on the lake," said John. "There may not be a good signal if he and the kids are on the lake."

"No," said Marie. "That's not it. Jim told me he got a new phone with a good signal."

"Well," John fished for answers. "Maybe he forgot his phone and left it at the camp."

"No John," said Marie. "Before we left, Jim told me he'd hang onto it so I could call anytime."

"Oh yeah, that's right," said John. "Well, I don't know why he's not answering Marie. But I bet everything is alright."

"I hope so," said Marie. "I hope the kids are having a good time."

She stared out the window and thought about the kids some more. She wondered if they had seen Champ while on the lake. The boys had been so excited to get the opportunity to see the dinosaur again.

"Tell you what," said John. "Let's turn on the radio to get our minds off the kids for a bit. I don't want you to sit and worry all day."

John turned on the radio and scanned through the stations. Only four could be found. He flipped between them for a bit, then settled on a country song that was a nice sing-along. It was too late though, the song ended and a stuffy sounding reporter began to talk.

"Now for today's local news," said the reporter. "Seth

and Edwin Slaughter are still at large. They are now believed to be somewhere in the area of Lake Champlain, perhaps near Button Bay State Park."

Marie's jaw dropped open. "That's where the kids are!" she shouted.

John swerved the car on the road. He straightened out and turned the radio up so he could listen.

"Seth, a former crime lord, recently escaped from prison to join Edwin, who is wanted for theft and kidnapping. Both men are believed to be armed and dangerous. The two were last seen at a prison in Waterbury, Vermont. They were there visiting another family member behind bars. They have since teased authorities with online Facetube videos such as this one."

Some of the audio from Seth's last Facetube video began to play. "It's been a disappointing day, but my Gramps isn't done yet. He still has to do a lot of work so we can catch this lake monster! Just stay tuned! I want to tell you one more thing. You'll never catch me coppers!"

Marie turned the radio off.

"John!" she exclaimed. "Jim won't answer the phone and that no good Edwin Slaughter is back at Lake Champlain!"

"Man," said John. "Can you believe our luck?"

Marie angrily stared at John. She was trying to contain herself. John noticed and swerved the car.

"What?" he asked.

Marie couldn't believe how dense her husband seemed to be. She wondered if he had been driving too long and was getting tired.

"Marie, you're all red! It's like there's steam pouring out of your nostrils. Calm down before you breathe fire on me or something!"

"I just might breathe fire!" she screamed. Then, calming down, she started tapping on her phone. "Just drive a little faster please. I'm going to call the cops and report that our children might be missing. I kept their phone number from last summer's visit, just in case."

Marie dialed the number and a phone rang on the other end of the line. A secretary answered and said all the officers were currently out of the office. The entire force was busy looking for Seth and Edwin.

Marie explained her problem. The secretary told her the police would keep their eyes open, but nothing else could be done yet. The kids had to be absent for a whole day before a missing persons report could be filed.

"Are you kidding me?" asked Marie. "But there are two criminals on the loose!"

The secretary said she understood, but it was the normal procedure.

Marie finished the call and hung up. She sat for a moment and stared at John, thinking.

He took a sideways glance at her and said, "I'm driving as fast as I can, honey. Any faster and I could get a ticket."

Marie still stared at him.

"I don't want to get into trouble Marie," said John.

She continued to stare. She figured she made John uncomfortable, but right now she didn't care. She had too much on her mind. She was trying to figure out if there was something she could do while they were driving. It was very possible the kids were okay, but then again, what if they had gotten into trouble? The boys were often full of mischief. They were even more so when a dinosaur was nearby.

John looked at Marie sideways. "Honey," he said. "We've been on the road for a while."

Marie woke up from her thought to listen.

"Mmm-hmm," she said.

John cleared his throat. "Well, I'm getting hungry," he said. "Any chance we could stop and grab something at the next Faster Burger?"

"Are you kidding?" asked Marie.

"No," said John. "I could really use a stop."

"You are just like the boys," said Marie.

"Does that mean we can stop?" asked John.

"Nope," said Marie.

She stared out the window and heard John sigh. She realized he was hungry, but their kids could be in trouble! There had to be something they could do! Well, John could drive, but what could Marie do? Then it hit her.

"Tracking!" she said out loud.

"What?" asked John.

"Tracking!" repeated Marie. "Remember how Noah got that GPS Tracker at the SwedishHomes store? You know, the one that doubled as a pocketknife? I'll track him to see if they're safe!"

Marie grabbed her phone and flipped through her apps.

"That's brilliant Marie," said John. "Like I said earlier, you are the brains behind this whole operation! You do all the heavy lifting."

"I know," said Marie. "And I know you love me John.

Just get us to Button Bay State Park."

John cleared his throat again. "Are you sure we can't stop honey?" he asked.

"Not a chance," said Marie.

CHAPTER 20
BURNT BY THE FIRE

"Noah," said Nathan. "I've got a problem."

"Shush," said Noah. "I'm thinking."

There had to be a way the Drakes could spoil Grandpa Edwin's plan to catch Champ. Last time they messed up the hunt by telling him to hit Champ's tail with a paddle. It was something Noah had remembered from Uncle Jim's first encounter with the lake monster. Uncle Jim had thought Champ's tail was a snake. He had hit it with a paddle, trying to kill it. Unfortunately Champ hit back and knocked Uncle Jim out of his boat. The same thing happened to Grandpa Edwin because Noah tricked him into doing the same thing as Uncle Jim. It ruined Edwin's plans to catch Champ.

Noah thought about the recipe for the bait. Seth Slaughter said it worked so well because Champ liked the smell of the fish. In the story from the Catholic Bible, Daniel used animal fat instead of fish guts. Then he mixed it together with tar and hair. A dragon's body couldn't digest the homemade hairball, but it couldn't spit it back up either. In the end, the dragon died and its body split open.

What if Noah could somehow change the recipe? Seth and Edwin were still cooking, so there was still time. What if Noah could mess it up and make the recipe not work? But how could he do it?

Maybe Noah could take the hair out of the recipe. Perhaps the bait would be more edible that way. The tar wasn't fit to eat, but maybe it wouldn't be as bad without the hair.

The bag of hair sat between Noah and the campfire. He looked at it. It was a huge black garbage bag with a variety of different colored hair spilling over the top.

"Where in the world did you get all that hair?" asked Noah.

"Huh?" asked Seth. "Oh, Gramps picked it up before he helped bust me out of jail. Apparently he'd been stockpiling it up from his local barber."

"Oh," said Noah. So it's human hair, he thought to himself. Noah had heard stories about people's hair catching fire, it ignites quickly. The hair doesn't really burn, but the oil on it does. That's why it lights so fast.

Noah had dealt with some of his own hair burning the last month. He had helped his dad light the gas pit for a barbecue dinner. That night the gas wouldn't ignite. Noah had a box of matches and must have used a hundred of them before the fire ever lit. When it did, the flames erupted with a small explosion. All the hair on the back of Noah's right hand instantly burned away from the sudden eruption of flames. It didn't hurt, but the scent of burnt hair stuck in his nose for a whole week.

So that was it, Noah needed to burn the hair to mess up the recipe. How could he do it though? Seth was an escaped prisoner and he currently had a gun. He'd probably shoot Noah, and his family, if they purposely kicked the bag of hair into the fire. There had to be another way to do it.

"Noah," whispered Nathan.

Noah tried to ignore his brother.

"Noah," he said a bit louder. "I gotta go to the bathroom."

Noah exploded, "You and your bathroom visits! You're always needing the bathroom!"

"But I gotta go," said Nathan.

Just then Noah stopped in his thoughts. That was it! That's how they could mess up the recipe. Nathan was accident-prone! Noah didn't have to kick the hair into the fire. He and Nathan could just look at it while going to use the bathroom. Given enough time, and maybe a little encouragement, Nathan would easily screw up something by accident! Noah looked at his brother. He didn't look happy. Who would be after being yelled at by their brother.

"Sorry Nathan," said Noah.

"No kidding!" said Nathan. "You really don't like me do you? You insult me, make fun of me and even yell at me."

"Nathan, I didn't mean to," said Noah.

"Yes you did," said Nathan. "All I said was I had to go to the bathroom. That's not my fault, and it's not my fault we're here! You act like I'm to blame for everything, but you had a part in us being here too! You're also to blame. You act like I can't do anything right, like I'm stupid. It doesn't matter what I do! Well I give up. I just wanted a brother that cared about me, but I give up. You don't have to worry about me anymore. I'll just go off to some corner and leave you alone."

Noah realized he went too far. The truth was, he did care about his brother. Sure, Nathan could be annoying, but he was still cool. Nathan wasn't stupid either. He didn't know as much about dinosaurs as Noah, but he did know a lot about the Bible. In fact, he might have known a little more about the Bible than Noah. It was part of his personality, and Noah liked it. He liked his brother. He didn't want their relationship to be like this, especially when some crazy escaped prisoner could kill them.

"Listen Nathan," said Noah. "I didn't mean to yell at you. I was trying to," he stopped and looked at Seth. Then he whispered, "I was trying to figure how to fix this. I think I know what to do."

"That's fine," said Nathan. He stared at Noah without emotion. "You're the perfect brother who doesn't do anything wrong. You just make your plans and I'll stay here with Norah and Uncle Jim."

"Nathan, it's not like that," said Noah.

"Whatever," said Nathan. He turned away and stared at the fire.

"Nathan, I'm sorry," said Noah. "I've been really mean

for a while. I don't know why. I just, I was just, I just haven't been using my head. I've been selfish and it's made me mean."

"You got that right," said Nathan. "You're unthinking, heartless and rude."

"Hang on," said Noah. "I'm not heartless."

"Well I'm not really feeling the love right now," said Nathan.

Noah sighed. "Yeah, you're right," he said. "I guess I have been heartless. I've been rude and, well, I'm sorry. Can you forgive me?" He held out his hand so they could shake on it.

Nathan looked at Noah with a grin. "Are you serious?" he asked.

"Of course I'm serious," said Noah.

"It's just that you're all business-like," said Nathan. "Like this is a binding contract or something."

"Hey," said Noah. "Being brothers is serious stuff. Don't leave me hanging."

Nathan pushed Noah's hand away and hugged him tightly.

"I forgive you," said Nathan. "I love you and I forgive you."

The two boys stood there hugging for a moment. Then Noah noticed Seth looking at them.

"Um, this is getting awkward," said Noah.

Nathan let go and smiled at his brother.

"I'm sorry for yelling at you Nathan," said Noah.

"Oh, that's alright," said Nathan. "I'm used to it. So what's your plan?"

"Just follow my lead," said Noah. He cleared his throat and addressed Seth Slaughter. "Excuse me sir, my brother has to go to the bathroom."

"Pick a tree," said Seth. "They're everywhere. Just don't go over there by my tent."

Noah nodded to Nathan, and pointed in a direction on the other side of the fire.

"Okay," said Nathan out loud. "I'll just go over here so I have a little privacy."

"No prob," said Seth. "But don't get any ideas about escaping. Even if you leave, I still have the rest of your family, and a gun." Seth smiled.

"No escaping," said Nathan. "I'm not escaping, just going to the bathroom."

As soon as Nathan walked away, Noah asked another question.

"I'm really interested in that bait for Champ," he said. "Could I take a look at it?"

"You really want to get that close?" asked Seth. "It smells horrible."

"Yeah, but I'd like to see what it looks like," said Noah.

"Suit yourself," said Seth. "But don't say I didn't warn you." He flipped through the pages of the magazine, but his eyes stayed on Noah and Nathan.

Noah walked over to the bubbling pot of fish guts. He tried to position himself next to the hair, so Nathan could stand next to it also. The stench from the pot was horrible. Noah gagged, but tried to keep his reflexes together until Nathan came back.

Nathan finished his business and walked towards Noah.

Noah motioned with his eyes to stand on the other side of the hair. Nathan did as Noah suggested and they both stared at the pot of simmering goo.

"Wow this stuff stinks," said Nathan.

Noah tried to talk, but only gagged. He stepped away from the smoke to get a breath, looking at the bag of hair between him and Nathan.

"I bet it won't smell any better when this hair gets put into it," said Nathan.

"I bet you're right," said Noah. He kicked at the bag of hair, like he was just checking it out.

"Don't get any ideas over there," said Seth.

"Huh?" asked Nathan.

"I said don't get any ideas." Seth stood up and began to hobble towards the boys.

"Oh, we're not trying to escape," said Nathan. "We're just looking at the hair." He bent down and picked up a hand full. "There's a lot in here! Red, grey, black. Edwin must have stopped at a lot of barber shops." He tossed the hair back into the bag.

That's when it happened. Nathan turned to walk back towards the camp, but his foot twisted on a large rock. He fell sideways and landed on top of the bag. Most of its contents launched, as if fired from a cannon, into the fire. Immediately the hair erupted into flames.

"No!" yelled Seth.

Nathan felt the heat from the flames hit his back. In a panic, he scrambled to his feet. He accidentally kicked the remaining bag into the fire as his feet found the ground.

"What are you doing?!" hollered Seth.

"I'm just trying to get away from the fire!" hollered Nathan. "It's hot!"

"Of course it's hot!" yelled Seth. "You burnt up all the hair!"

"What?" asked Nathan. "I did?" He looked at the fire and noticed the bag of hair. It was melting into flames. "Oh no," he said. "I'm sorry. I didn't mean to do it."

"I know," said Seth. "I can see from the other side of the camp that you're clumsy."

"Well that's not my fault," said Nathan.

"No, it's not," said Noah. He stood beside his brother to help defend him from Seth. "Why'd you put that bag of hair so close to the fire anyway? Don't you know that hair burns?"

Seth stood and put his hands on his hips. He cocked his head sideways while looking at the boys. He looked like he suspected they did the whole thing on purpose. An ornery smile appeared on his face.

"I don't know how, but I get the feeling that you planned that out."

"What?" asked Noah sheepishly.

"Honestly mister," said Nathan. "It was an accident. I didn't mean to do it."

"Sure," said Seth. "I've heard that before."

CHAPTER 21
CHAMP IS HOOKED

Seth was recording a Facetube video when Grandpa Edwin returned from the boat. Edwin was furious and Seth got the whole reaction on tape.

"You mean to tell me that my bait is ruined?" hollered Edwin. "Plus those meddling Drake kids are back?!"

"Keep yelling Gramps," said Seth. "This makes great video!"

Edwin tore off his shoe and threw it at Seth. It hit the smart phone and nearly knocked it from his hands. "I'll give you good video, you dummy! Don't you realize who these kids are?"

"Yeah, they're some nosey boys who smelled that awful fish bait cooking," said Seth. "They just wanted to see what it was, but they heard us talking so I couldn't let them go."

"Seth," said Edwin. "They're the same kids that botched up our operation last time. Last time we tried to catch Champ they messed it up, and they've already messed it up again this time! I can't get any more hair to finish the bait! I don't even know where I'd begin to get more hair around here."

Seth pointed the camera at his head and said, "I'd give you mine if I could, but I don't have any." He ran a hand over the top of his head, "It's smooth and suave."

"Oh my gosh," said Edwin, rolling his eyes.

"How about the kids?" asked Seth. "Can you use their hair?"

Edwin looked at the kids, thinking. "No," he said. "It's not enough. I'm going to need a lot more."

"So what do we do?" asked Seth, looking into the camera. "Grab our guns and go after Champ in a blaze of glory?" He was hamming it up for the camera.

"Are you going to try shooting Champ again?" said Uncle Jim. "Tell me you didn't dredge up that old Gatling gun from the lake."

"No you dummy," said Grandpa Edwin. "That gun is lost forever." He grabbed Seth's hand and pointed the smartphone at himself. "That's the kind of gun-power we'd need to take Champ out, a Gatling gun or something like a machine gun. We don't have anything like that."

"But Gramps," said Seth.

Edwin ignored him and kept talking. "Even if we had

166

that kind of gun power, it could get us into more trouble with the law."

"But Grandpa," said Seth.

"No, let's keep it simple," said Grandpa Edwin. "We'll try the bait, it's all we have but it should still attract that old dragon. We'll bait the Slaughter Hook and go fishing, and then we'll use the winch to reel in Champ. The bait may not kill him, but it can still catch him."

Seth turned away from Grandpa and pointed the phone at himself. "That's a stupid plan," he whispered into the phone. "It's stupid. What do we do with Champ once we catch him?"

Grandpa Edwin began loading up the bait to take to the boat. Seth looked at him and then back at the phone. "I guess that's it for now Facetube friends!" he said. "I'll let you know how the Champ-fishing goes! Oh, and one more thing, you'll never catch me coppers!"

He ended the video, grabbed his rifle and rounded up the Drake family. Grandpa Edwin led everyone towards the lakeside and then down a trail towards the boat. Seth limped along in the rear, keeping an eye on the kids and Uncle Jim.

"Don't get any funny ideas," said Seth. "You can't all escape at the same time. If one of you gets away, I may have to hurt the rest of the family for your stupidity."

Nathan turned and looked at Seth. "That's not fair," he said.

"It is too fair," said Seth, pointing the rifle towards Nathan. "I'm the one with the gun. That means you have to do what I say."

"Or what?" asked Nathan.

"Duh Nathan," said Noah, turning around. "Or else he'll shoot us."

"Yeah," said Seth. "What he said."

"You wouldn't dare," said Nathan.

A shadow crept over Seth's face. "Don't be so sure," he said. "I'm a convict. I broke out of prison. I'm not afraid to hurt some kid for talking back to me."

Nathan's eyes grew really big. "Wow, you need Jesus mister. You need to get saved."

Nathan's boldness caught Seth off guard. Nobody had ever told him that he needed Jesus. He shook his head in an attempt to clear it. "Just," he stuttered. "Just get going. Catch up to your family and get on the boat."

Nathan turned and caught up to his family. The trail caught up to a clearing overlooking the lake. At the water's edge was an old, dilapidated wooden dock with a small yacht tied to the end.

"That's your boat?" asked Noah.

Grandpa Edwin turned and said, "Yep! Seth has some good connections!"

"That's no boat," said Uncle Jim. "That's a luxury cruiser! We don't see many of those on this part of the lake."

"Yeah," said Seth. "We want to keep a low profile, but it's nice to have the best of what's available."

"We get to ride the boat?" asked Norah.

Uncle Jim looked at the little girl, trying to keep a smile on his face. "Yes we do," he said. "These nice guys are taking us for a boat ride!"

"Unca' Jim," said Norah. "These aren't nice guys."

Uncle Jim smiled at her blunt honesty. "I know," he said.

"Just stay close to me and we'll be okay."

"Okay," said Norah.

Edwin lugged the bait up to the main level of the boat and then drug it towards the rear.

"Go on," Seth said to the Drakes. "Head back there with Gramps."

The Drake family followed Grandpa Edwin while Seth stumbled along behind. When the group got to the rear of the deck, Seth pointed to a long, cushioned seat along the backside of the cabin. "Sit down and stay there, while Grandpa and I get this thing going."

In no time, the boat launched out toward the center of the lake and began to slowly glide across the water.

"Okay Seth," said Grandpa Edwin. "Let's set the bait!"

Edwin loosed a length of line from the winch and lifted the Slaughter Hook up to the deck. Then he clumped a large chunk of bait into a bit of netting to hold it together. He stuck the bait onto the hook and gently lowered it over the side. A small breeze blew at Edwin's face and he took a deep breath.

"Here we go Daddy," he said. "Time to catch Champ again!"

"You'll never get him," said Noah. "He won't fall for something like that."

"Oh yes he will," said Grandpa Edwin. "He likes this stuff, and soon he'll smell it under that water." He shouted for emphasis, "Then Wham! We got him!"

"It can't be that easy," said Noah.

"I don't know," said Seth. "One of the babies came towards the shore the last time we were cooking it on the fire. I think it might be pretty easy."

"It is!" said Grandpa Edwin. "It's easy as apple pie. Champ will grab onto this hook, I'll push the button on this winch and then he'll get reeled up to the boat!"

"But Gramps," said Seth. "How do you know when he's on the hook?"

Suddenly the yacht jerked, as if it had anchored onto something below the water.

"That's how I know," said Edwin. He punched a button on the winch and it began to whir, pulling up the line.

"Shoot, we didn't get him." said Edwin.

"How do you know?" asked Noah.

"Because Champ is big!" said Edwin. "If you thought that yank was something, wait till Champ grabs onto the hook. That will be a real struggle!"

"Holy cow!" said Seth. "I gotta record this! I totally forgot!"

Edwin let out a sigh and then lifted the hook over the edge of the boat.

Seth turned on his phone and began another broadcast.

"Hi Facetubers!" he said. "It's go time! We're on the water and ready to catch Champ. We've already had a bit of action. Something huge just stole the bait from our hook, but we're not done yet!"

He pointed the camera at Edwin Slaughter.

"See?" said Seth. "Gramps is baiting the hook as we speak!"

"Oh Seth," said Grandpa Edwin. "I can't live with you and I can't live without," he paused for a moment. "No, I can live without you. You're not doing anything to help!"

Edwin added another chunk of bait to the hook and lowered it into the water.

"Yes I am Gramps," said Seth. "I'm advertising! You won't have to do anything now to try to sell Champ. The world will see it!"

"You know what?" said Edwin. "You're right! That's a good idea Seth! I think that's the first one you've had yet!"

"Gee, thanks Gramps!" said Seth. "Hey, wait a minute. The first good idea?"

Edwin ignored him. He stopped the winch from lowering and let the hook troll along behind the boat.

"You're not going to catch Champ!" said Noah. "And even if you do, what will you do then?"

"What do we do?" repeated Edwin. "Why, we'll pull him to the shore. That's what we'll do, you dummy!"

Seth pointed the camera at himself and quietly muttered. "See? I told you it was a stupid plan! What do you do with a living dinosaur once you pull it to the shore? Get eaten for dessert?"

Noah stuck his head into the frame of the video and muttered, "No kidding! Grandpa Edwin isn't very good at planning these things out!"

Just then the boat jerked to a stop. Edwin had been ready and was hanging onto the rail. Seth wasn't ready. He flew forward against the cushioned seat on the rear of the cabin, nearly smashing Norah.

"We got him!" hollered Edwin. "We got him!" He punched the button on the winch and the motor began to whir.

"No way!" hollered Nathan.

171

"Yes way," said Grandpa Edwin.

"Not again," said Uncle Jim.

"I smashed my toe!" hollered Seth, now lying on the cushion of the seat. He held up his phone and asked, "Could you record Champ for me?"

Noah grabbed the phone and leapt to the rear guardrail overlooking the water. He pointed the camera towards the water, where the line from the winch was growing very tight.

"We've got something alright!" said Noah.

"It has to be him this time!" hollered Edwin. A crazed look came over his face. "It has to be that old dragon! We've got him this time."

The winch was now whining, but continued to pull the line. The yacht began to pull backwards, being drug by the lake monster.

"Are you sure we have Champ?" asked Noah. "Or does Champ have us?"

The winch continued to whine. It was still pulling, but very slowly. Smoke began to rise from the motor.

"It's the hair," said Seth. "It won't die without the hair. We gotta shoot and kill it."

"No," said Grandpa Edwin. "It's fine! We've got him this time!"

Then, without warning, the boat was loosed. The line with Champ went slack and the winch set in motion again, pulling the line in. The boat started moving forward again and a breeze picked back up.

"What happened?" asked Grandpa Edwin.

The line on the winch surfaced above the water. The

hook was still attached, kind of. It was now bent and broken in half. The sharp end of the hook was gone, and so was the bait and Champ. The winch automatically stopped when the hook reached the top.

Noah pointed the camera phone at himself and spoke. "You saw it right here. Grandpa Edwin caught something huge, probably Champ. I don't know what else could pull a yacht like this backwards, especially with the engine still running! But the old hook broke! Part of it is gone and Champ is on the loose!"

"What happens now?" asked Nathan.

"What happens now?" repeated Seth. He slid off the bench cushion and lifted the top, revealing a storage compartment. Inside was enough artillery to equip a small army. Seth grabbed a rifle with an extremely large double-barrel. He turned to look into the phone camera that Noah had been holding. "I'll tell you what happens now. We shoot it! You'll never catch me coppers."

Seth reached for the phone and stopped the recording.

Chapter 22
The Long Drive

John and Marie Drake were making good time on the drive. Marie finally admitted that she was hungry, so the two made a quick stop at Faster Burger, John's favorite fast food joint. Back on the highway, the drive was long, but they were getting closer to the little tracking beacon Marie had found on her phone.

"Has there been any change in their location honey?" asked John.

Marie jumped. She had been staring out the window. She looked at her phone, tapped at the app and waited for it to load.

Up till now the tracking beacon had stayed next to the lake. John guessed it was the boy's campsite since the beacon hadn't moved. Marie said she didn't like it being stuck in one place. She said the lack of movement scared her.

"It's moved!" said Marie. "Not far, but it's now in the middle of the lake. What could that mean?"

"Hmm," said John.

"Are they swimming?" asked Marie. "What if they're in trouble? What if they've drowned?"

"It's okay Marie," said John. "Don't jump to conclusions. They must be on a boat or something. I don't think the GPS would work under the water if they had drowned. The boys are probably just fishing on a boat."

"Fishing, and in a boat," said Marie, "Yeah, you're probably right."

Marie stared out the window and John continued to drive. He hoped he was right. He hoped the boys were just fishing. Under different circumstances John would enjoy this trip. He liked long drives through new places, but it was hard to enjoy this drive. John was worried. He wouldn't let Marie know, but he was worried for his kids.

The boys ran into trouble during their last trip to Lake Champlain. John and Marie had been with them for that trip. They escaped okay, but John never dreamed it would happen again. This time he and Marie weren't there to help. Plus, Norah was with the boys for this trip.

John didn't want to think about that. He didn't like the thought of his kids being hurt. He took a deep breath. Maybe a good conversation would take his mind somewhere better.

"You know," said John, "that class on biblical creation, at the homeschool conference, was pretty interesting."

Marie looked at him, dumbfounded. John picked the right conversation. This one would probably last a while. Generally John had a hard time with the earth being created about six-thousand years ago by God. He believed in God, and he believed God created everything, but he also thought evolution had a place in things too. Marie knew John's thoughts on the subject and wanted him to attend the class. She had hoped it would help John understand what the boys were learning in their study at home.

"What did you say?" asked Marie.

John smiled. "I said it was interesting."

"What did you find interesting?" asked Marie.

"Well, you know," said John. "It was about making class more exciting for your kids."

"Yeah," said Marie. "What about it?"

"Well they suggested focusing on things that kids like, like dinosaurs," said John.

"Hmm," said Marie. "Did they say what to focus on with dinosaurs?"

John shifted a little in his seat. He was still uncomfortable with this subject, but it did get his mind off the kids.

"They spoke about how dinosaurs were created by God in the last six-thousand years. They said some could still be alive today."

"And you believe that?" asked Marie.

John exhaled, "I'm not saying that. I'm just saying it was

interesting. They did have some neat ways to prove it though. They spoke about how it's hard to believe dinosaurs went extinct, millions of years ago, when there are tales about them in modern history."

Marie smiled. "So, what kind of tales did they share?"

John shifted a little more in his seat. "Well, dinosaur fossils weren't discovered and named until about two hundred years ago. But there were stories of dinosaur sightings long before, and some since then. Did you know that an Arizona newspaper printed a story about a winged monster in 1890? The story described something a lot like a pterodactyl."

"Really?" asked Marie. "No, I've never heard that before."

"Well, you've heard of the Thunderbird, right?" asked John.

"You mean the sports car made by Ford?" asked Marie.

"Well, yes," said John, "but that car was named after the real thunderbird. It was a legendary creature that terrorized American Indians. Maybe that's the same pterodactyl that was written about in the Arizona newspaper."

"That's interesting," said Marie.

"Yeah, they brought up dinosaur legends from all over the world. There's St. George. He's the patron saint of England and Romania. He was a Roman soldier who slew a dragon."

"I've heard of him," said Marie. "We read about him in the kid's history book this year. They say he came to a town that was sacrificing a princess to the dragon. The sacrifice was supposed to be how the people saved the town from the monster. St. George saved the day by killing it."

"That's right," said John. "And you've probably heard about Marco Polo."

"Yes," said Marie. "We studied Marco Polo in school this year! He explored China during the 1200's and wrote about it."

"That's right," said John. "Did you know he wrote about dragons?"

"Yes!" said Marie. "He wrote about how the Chinese Emperor raised dragons. They were used to lead his chariot during parades. Apparently the Emperor even hired a dragon feeder to take care of them."

"He wrote more too," said John. "Marco Polo described school bus-sized serpents, with two legs in the front and a big claw in the back. He described how they were killed and then used for medicine and stuff."

"Cool," said Marie.

"Yeah, doesn't it sound like some kind of medieval movie?" asked John.

Marie smiled at him. "What else did you learn?" she asked.

"Hmm," said John. "They spoke about John of Damascus. He was a church leader that wrote about science and religion. He wrote about how dragons were real and originally named by Adam."

"Seriously?" said Marie.

"I guess so," said John. "He said dragons were born small, but grew up to be huge. He also dismissed legends that said dragons were smarter than humans. He said those were just fantasies."

179

"You sure do remember a lot from this conference," said Marie.

"Yeah, I guess I do," said John. "They brought up modern legends too, like the Loch Ness Monster. People have seen it for years, especially after a highway was built near Loch Ness. Every year, new people say they've seen it."

"Did they say anything about Champ?" asked Marie.

John felt his ears turn red. He didn't talk for a bit. The conversation was getting a little too close for his comfort. His boys, and his brother, all said they had seen Champ. John wanted to believe them, but it was just too fantastic. Could he really believe dinosaurs, or dragons, were alive today?

"John," Marie interrupted his thought. "Did they talk about Champ?"

"A little," said John. "After talking about the Loch Ness Monster, they said we had a local lake monster in Lake Champlain. That was it."

Marie stared at him. "That's a lot of information," she said. "Marco Polo, St. George, John of Damascas and Champ."

"It is a lot of information," said John.

She continued staring at him and finally asked, "Do you think there's any truth to it?"

There it was. Marie put John on the spot. He was hoping the conversation wouldn't turn this way. Why did he start talking about this again?

"Marie," said John. "I don't know. I mean, our kids say they saw something, but I don't know. They were so excited about seeing it too, about seeing Champ I mean. It's just so

180

hard to grasp! If there really were lake monsters in Lake Champlain, if there really were dinosaurs alive today, wouldn't more people know about it?"

"Maybe they're all like your brother Jim," said Marie. "He's afraid to tell people. He's worried they'll think he's nuts."

"But, wouldn't more people know about it?" asked John. "Why haven't we seen pictures and video?"

"There are pictures and video," said Marie. "But most of them just look like a log floating down the lake. If a person doesn't believe dinosaurs exist, why would they believe a picture of a log is really a dinosaur?"

"Exactly," said John. "That's exactly my point."

"So does that mean your brother Jim, and your two boys, are lying?" asked Marie.

"No," said John. "That's not what I'm saying."

"Then what are you saying?" asked Marie.

"It's just," stuttered John. "Why does science seem to ignore it if it's true? If there really are dinosaurs today, why can't we read about them in modern science books?"

Marie sighed. John knew she wanted him to believe in Champ. He knew she hoped he would believe his boys and his brother. But how could it be true?

"I guess that's a fair question," said Marie. "Why would science ignore the history books and the testimonies of people that say they've seen them? What is there to gain in ignoring the evidence?"

The Long Drive

CHAPTER 23
SETH ON THE RAMPAGE

"You can't shoot Champ!" shouted Noah.

"Watch me," said Seth. "And you meddling kids better stay out of my way if you know what's good for you!"

"Sit down Noah," said Uncle Jim. "He means business."

"Mr. Edwin, you can't let him shoot Champ!" cried Noah. "It's a legendary creature! It's a relic, and it's protected by law!"

"Law, shmaw," said Seth. "Who cares about the law? Now sit down like you were told."

Seth shoved Noah into the seat with his family.

Edwin Slaughter was still standing at the rail, rooted to

the same spot. His jaw hung open. He looked like he was in shock.

A loud cry came from under the water. It sounded like the cry of a whale, except it was angry and sharp.

"Uh oh," said Noah. "You've done it now."

Seth pulled what looked like a hand-held cannon from the artillery. A large metal arrow with a huge tip was loaded inside.

"Is that a harpoon?" asked Nathan.

"I don't know," said Seth. "But it looks pretty cool, doesn't it?"

He threw the cannon over his shoulder, carrying it like a book bag. "It's time for me to win this trophy for Grandpa Edwin," he said.

Another cry from Champ was heard from the front of the boat. Seth grabbed his double-barrel rifle and walked towards the noise.

"We have to do something," said Noah, looking at his family.

"But what?" asked Uncle Jim. "They have guns and we're supposed to sit still."

"Plus Mr. Edwin looks like he had a stroke or something," said Nathan.

The family looked at Edwin. He was still standing, frozen.

"Edwin?" asked Uncle Jim. "Are you alright?"

Edwin didn't move.

"Listen," said Nathan, "you're not being very Christian."

Grandpa Edwin's head jerked.

"What are you doing?" asked Noah.

"Well," said Nathan, "He's not acting very Christian."

Gunshots rang out from the front of the boat. It was incredibly loud and the sound caused everyone to jump, except Grandpa Edwin. He was still rooted to the spot. Uncle Jim and the kids looked at one another.

"Wait a minute," said Noah. "I have an idea. Perhaps we don't have to stop Seth from killing Champ."

"And let Champ die?" asked Nathan.

"No," said Noah, lowering his voice. "Maybe Mr. Edwin can stop Seth."

"I can't imagine that," said Nathan.

"Listen," Noah said quietly. "We could try to get the two Slaughters to fight. If things go well, Edwin will stop Seth for us!"

"I don't know," said Uncle Jim. "I don't trust either one of them."

"It's worth a try though," said Noah. "Don't you think? And this way, none of us have to be in the line of fire! Maybe Edwin and Seth would take each other out."

"That doesn't sound very nice," said Uncle Jim.

"That don't sound nice," repeated Norah.

"Do you have a better plan?" asked Noah.

There was a short silence. Uncle Jim shrugged his shoulders and Norah shook her head.

"Alright then," said Nathan, "what do we do?"

"You keep talking to him Nathan. Preach to him," said Noah. "You got a head jerk before. See if you can get more."

"Okay," said Nathan. He took a deep breath and spoke up to Edwin. "You're not being very Christian, Mr. Edwin. You're not walking in love."

Grandpa Edwin blinked his eyes.

"I think he's coming around," said Noah. "Keep going!"

"If you were a true Christian, you'd act more like Jesus!"

Grandpa Edwin turned to look at Nathan. "What are you talking about?" he asked. "I've been a Christian all my life!"

Nathan's jaw fell open.

"I was raised in the church and I still go every Sunday," said Edwin. "Well, I was going every Sunday." His entire body now turned to face the boys. "I know all ten of the Commandments, plus I take communion. How can you say I'm not a Christian?"

"Because you're not acting like one," said Nathan.

"What, in God's name, are you talking about boy?" asked Grandpa Edwin.

"If you're a Christian, a follower of Jesus Christ, why don't you act like it?" asked Nathan. "Jesus said, if you follow Him, you would do what He did."

"What's your point?" asked Grandpa Edwin.

"My point is that Jesus never held anyone up with a gun," said Nathan. "But you have, twice now! Why are you being so mean? Why are you trying to kill Champ?"

"I'm not being mean," said Edwin.

"Yes you are!" yelled Nathan.

"Well," said Edwin, "If I am, it's because you meddling kids keep getting in the way!"

"Then stop being so selfish," said Noah. "Stop trying to save that dinosaur for yourself! All you want to do is take its life and cash in on some reward!"

"Yes I do!" said Edwin. "What's wrong with that? I've worked my whole life trying to live the American dream. I had a home, a wife and kids. Where did it get me? Nowhere, I'm old, broke and tired. But I still want that old dragon, and I'm tired of waiting for it. I want it now!"

"Even if it means killing a couple of kids because they're in your way?" asked Noah.

Edwin stared at the boys, but he didn't answer.

"You see?" said Nathan. "Jesus wouldn't do that! I told you, you're not a Christian."

"Listen here boy," said Grandpa Edwin. "Everyone chases after the things they want, the desires of their heart. It doesn't matter if they're Christian, it's the way of the world! So don't talk about things you don't understand."

"But I do understand," argued Nathan, "and you're going about it the wrong way!"

"Then how do I do it?" asked Edwin.

"The Bible says to delight yourself in God and He'll give you the desires of your heart," said Nathan. "God will provide what you really want Mr. Edwin. That's His plan! That's His way, and His way is better! It's easier."

"Yeah," said Noah. "He doesn't hold a gun to people's heads to make it happen."

Grandpa Edwin took a deep breath. "Look here boys," he said. "I'm old and I'm tired. I'm through waiting. I want to take what I want, and I want to do it now."

"But Mr. Edwin," said Nathan. "The Bible says that God clothes the flowers in the valley and He feeds the birds of the air. If he cares about the flowers and the birds, don't you think he cares about you and what you want?"

"Yeah," said Noah. "Do you think He loves them more than He loves you?"

"No, I guess not," said Grandpa Edwin. "But how does that help me get Champ?"

"You don't need to get him," said Nathan. "God can do that for you."

"So I don't do anything?!" asked Edwin. "That doesn't make any sense."

"This is all you need to do," said Nathan. "Love the Lord your God with all your heart, all your mind and all your soul. Also, love your neighbor like you love yourself. Those are the only rules Jesus gave us to obey. If you follow those rules, you're proving to God that you love Him and trust Him to take care of you."

"But what about Champ?" asked Grandpa Edwin.

"Give God what He wants," said Nathan. "Do that and He'll help you get Champ. If you keep trying to get Champ your way, then you'll keep breaking all the rules! When you want what other people have, and you steal or murder to get it, you're not obeying God. Instead you're doing what the devil does and he's going to hell. Is Champ really worth breaking God's commands to act like the devil?"

"What? You think I'm going to hell for trying to catch Champ?" asked Edwin. "You just told me that God loved me. What, do I have to follow a bunch of rules to get His love?"

"No, Mr. Edwin." said Nathan. "God loves you no matter what. But it breaks His heart if you don't love Him. And if you love Him, you'll do things His way."

"So I'm breaking God's heart?" asked Grandpa Edwin.

"Really?"

Nathan rested his head in his hands and took a deep breath. "Mr. Edwin, did your father love you?" he asked.

"Of course he loved me," said Edwin.

"Did you love him?"

"Yes, I loved my Dad very much!" said Edwin. "He was good to me and loved me, and I loved him."

"When he asked you to do something, did you do it?" asked Nathan.

Edwin scratched his head. "Yes," he said.

"Did you do your chores and school like he would have wanted?" asked Nathan.

"Of course!" said Edwin.

"Why?" asked Nathan. "Did you think he wouldn't love you if you didn't do them? Were you trying to earn your Dad's love?"

"Of course not, you dummy," said Edwin. "He's my daddy. He loved me no matter what."

"Then why did you do what he asked you to do?" asked Nathan.

"Because," said Edwin. "I loved him."

"And that's why you obey God's commandments," said Nathan. "That's why you do things His way. God loves you no matter what. But do you love Him?"

"I think I do," said Grandpa Edwin.

"If you do, then you'll follow His rules," said Nathan. "Christians are saved by grace, but that doesn't mean we get to do whatever we want. No, we follow God's rules. We show God that we are Christians by doing what He wants. Are you really a Christian Mr. Edwin?"

Edwin opened his mouth to talk, but Seth interrupted him. "No he's not a Christian, ya dummy!" Seth had come back when no one was looking. "Can't you tell that by what he's doing? He's never been a Christian, at least not while I've known him. He looks out for himself, no matter who gets in the way. And you know what, I think he's got it right. Maybe it's just the Slaughter way of thinking, but I think he's right. Take what you can, when you can. Who wants to be a Christian anyway?"

"I do," said Edwin.

Seth laughed. "You sure have a funny way of showing it Gramps."

CHAPTER 24
TRACKING THE KIDS

Thwapp! The tree limb hit John in the face so hard that he stumbled backwards.

"Marie, hang on!" he said. "That really hurt!"

Marie turned and looked at her husband. "Oh man up!" she said. "We're nearly there. It's just a little further down the hill."

"I know," said John, "but can you take it easy on letting the limbs go? That last one nearly bush-whacked my head off."

"Oh come on you big baby," said Marie.

She and John had arrived at Lake Champlain. They had

watched the tracking beacon move for a while, but then it stopped in the middle of the lake. They were getting close to the spot. They had abandoned the car a mile or so back and then followed a well-beaten path. They passed a really cool looking tree that was bowing low to the ground. Not long afterward they turned into the brush towards the beacon on the lake.

"I wish they'd just answer the stupid phone," said John. "Why won't they answer?"

The sound of gunshots came from the lake ahead of them. Marie froze and looked at John.

"Oh no. Oh no!" she said.

"It'll be okay," said John. "It's going to be okay. Let's use your phone to call the cops though. Maybe they can track us here if we find the Slaughters."

Marie nodded. She handed her phone to John.

"But what about the tracking program?" he asked.

"We're nearly there," said Marie. "We don't need it anymore. Make the call."

The two continued to walk while John dialed the police line. As the phone rang, he and Marie reached a shallow shore of rocks that overlooked the lake. John nearly fell in the water. He hadn't realized they were that close. Ahead of them, in the middle of the water, sat a large yacht. They could hear voices coming from the boat.

John spoke into the phone. "Hello, this is John Drake. I'm at Lake Champlain and I believe my kids have been taken against their will. Yes, we've tracked them here with a GPS signal."

Marie kept her eyes locked on the boat, hoping to see

one of the three kids or Uncle Jim. She could still hear talking, but it was low and unclear. Then, suddenly she heard Nathan, speaking clearly.

"You're not being very Christian Mr. Edwin," said Nathan. "You're not walking in love. If you were a true Christian, you'd act more like Jesus!"

Nathan's voice washed Marie in a mixture of emotion. She was excited to finally find her kids. She was relieved to know where they were. She was also terrified, because Nathan was speaking to Edwin Slaughter.

Next to Marie, John spoke into the phone. He sounded aggravated. "I know you're looking for Edwin Slaughter," said John. "I think we may have found him."

John looked at Marie and mouthed the words "They're not listening."

From on the boat Marie heard Nathan yell, "Yes you are!" Then she heard Edwin Slaughter yell back, "it's because you meddling kids keep getting in the way!"

Marie clenched her hand into a fist. She needed to help her kids! Maybe she could swim to the boat. She took her shoes off, but hesitated.

"Well, no," John stammered into the phone. "It hasn't been twenty-four hours, but..." he stopped talking. The officer had cut him off.

Marie couldn't stand it anymore. She ripped the phone from John's hands and spoke into it. Her voice trembled with fear and anger.

"This is Marie Drake and I can hear my kids talking to Edwin Slaughter! They addressed him by name. I also heard that criminal yelling at them. We even heard gunshots! We are standing on the side of the lake, helpless! Now either you need to get here and catch this lawbreaker or I'm going to swim to his boat and do something stupid!"

"Now that's more substantial," said an officer from the other end of the phone. "I need you to stay on this line. We have officers up and down Lake Champlain looking for the Slaughters. There's even a patrol in the sky. Please, don't swim to the boat. You could make the situation worse, especially if they have a gun."

"Okay," said Marie. "What do we do? Our kids are in danger."

"Ma'am," said the officer, "I have an idea. Give me a moment to talk with my superior. Can you hang on for a moment?"

Marie took a deep breath. "You have one minute."

The officer put down the phone. Marie looked at John. "He's checking on something," she said.

"Well," said John. "I'm swimming to that boat before you do, Marie." He looked at her sternly. Marie smiled.

From on the boat came Noah's voice. He was yelling. "All you want to do is take its life and cash in on some reward!"

Marie breathed in sharply.

"Yes I do!" shouted back Edwin. "What's wrong with that?"

Apparently John decided to take action. He strode into the water, but stumbled on a rock and fell in. Marie walked over and helped him up.

On the other end of the phone, the officer began to speak.

"Are you still there Ma'am?" the officer asked.

"Yes," said Marie.

"Okay, don't move," said the officer. "We're tracking your phone right now. A team is on its way as we speak."

"Beep," went Marie's phone. The battery was going dead.

"Ummm," she said to the officer. "I need you to hurry. My phone is going dead."

Chapter 25
The Final Faceoff

"I have a funny way of showing I'm a Christian?" asked Grandpa Edwin. "What do you mean by that?"

"I mean I never thought you were a Christian," said Seth. "You don't act like it."

"I helped you escape from prison," said Edwin. "I drove you away in my car, I gave you a camp to rest at and I even fed you!"

"You didn't do those things for me Gramps," said Seth. "You did those things because you needed someone to help you catch Champ. You knew you couldn't do it on your own, so you went out of your way to find someone who

197

could help."

"But I haven't had any help!" said Grandpa Edwin. "I've had to do everything on my own!"

"Here we go again," said Seth.

"All you've done is sit on your backside," said Edwin. "You play with your phone and you gripe about your toe!"

"Then why don't you help with my toe?!" hollered Seth.

"What else can I do?" asked Edwin. "There's not much I can do for an injured toe. Instead, I let you rest."

"And you griped about it the whole time," said Seth.

"I suppose you're right," said Grandpa Edwin. He rubbed his eyes for an awkward moment and then paused to look at Nathan. "Perhaps I'm not being a good Christian."

Seth tilted his head to one side and looked at Grandpa Edwin. He looked like a confused dog.

"Well," said Uncle Jim. "It sounds like this is the perfect time to change."

Grandpa Edwin nodded his head. "I guess you're right," he said. "I should do things a little different. You know what? I'll start by letting you guys go."

Seth's jaw slackened as he continued to watch, his head was still cocked sideways.

"Now you're talking!" said Noah.

"Now you talkin'," repeated Norah.

The Drake family stood up. They were ready to get off the Slaughters' boat. The boys high-fived each other and Uncle Jim picked up Norah.

Seth woke up from his stupor. He strode over to the arsenal of guns and picked up a pistol. Pointing it at the family, he shouted, "Sit down!"

The Drake family immediately took their seats.

"I don't know what's going on here, but I don't like it." said Seth. "Nobody has cared to ask for my opinion, so I think it's time I've made it known. We're going to catch that Champ, one way or another. And since Gramps' way didn't work, then I guess it's time to give my way a shot." He cocked his pistol for emphasis and then laughed an evil laugh. Everyone stared at him in surprise. It seemed Seth's true colors were shining through.

"What do you say we broadcast this to the world?" asked Seth. He turned on his phone and began a live stream on Facetube. "Helloooooo subscribers! The party is just getting started here on Lake Champlain!" He let out a shout, lifted the pistol into the air and pulled the trigger. The ear splitting sound of a shot rang out. "Oh yeah!" said Seth.

Nathan looked at Noah and mouthed the words, "What do we do?" Noah shrugged his shoulders while Uncle Jim gave Nathan a stern look and mouthed the words, "Nothing Nathan. You do nothing."

Seth had now moved to the second level, where he could steer and control the boat. The sound of the throttle shifting into forward was heard and the boat began to move. Then Seth began talking to his camera.

"You see," said Seth, "my Gramps is distracted by these meddling kids. They've been busy talking about God and church and religion. All the while Champ got away! We can't let him go like that! We got to get him! The good news is that I saw where he went."

Edwin sighed to himself. His grandson Seth was so focused on his video that he was no longer paying attention to Edwin and the so-called 'meddling kids.' Edwin walked towards the Drake family and lifted the seat cushion that was next to them. His eyes searched through the arsenal of guns.

"What are you doing?" asked Nathan.

But Grandpa Edwin ignored him. He rummaged through the guns, looking. After a moment, he said "Get up" to the Drake family.

Everyone's eyes were huge in shock. Nathan jumped up, but then stumbled and did a face plant onto the floor. Edwin walked over to him.

"You can't do it Mr. Edwin!" said Nathan. "You can't continue helping Seth!"

Edwin stared at Nathan, then he bent down and helped him to his feet. "I'm not helping Seth," he said. "I'm helping you. There's no reason to be afraid."

"But I thought you were looking for a gun," said Nathan.

Edwin looked towards the stockpile of guns. "Oh that?" he asked. "I'm just looking for a life preserver. You need to get off this boat."

A collective sigh was heard between Noah, Nathan and Uncle Jim.

"You're helping us?" asked Nathan.

"You helping us?" repeated Norah.

Grandpa Edwin smiled. "Yes," he said. "I'm trying to love my neighbors, but we need to find some life preservers first." He lifted the seat cushion the Drakes had been sitting on. "Jackpot," he said, and he handed a pile of orange life vests to the kids.

Behind the wheel of the boat, Seth could still be heard

narrating his Facetube broadcast. He had no clue what Edwin and the Drakes were doing.

"Now I'm going to point the camera forward so you can see where we're going," said Seth. "When Champ took off, he came to the water's surface to look at our boat. He looked at me and let out an interesting cry. I think he was mad at me. He sounded like a whale. You know, like they sound on television? Then Champ turned away and went towards that bend up ahead."

The Drake family was nearly done putting on their life preservers. Grandpa Edwin even found an orange emergency raft that could inflate within seconds. He pulled the cord and, with a "fwoop" sound, the raft was ready to be used. Edwin swung a section of the guardrail outwards, like a gate, so the raft could launch overboard. Then he moved the raft onto the edge. The Drake family took their seats inside.

"Thanks for helping us Mr. Edwin," said Nathan.

"You guys take care of yourself," said Edwin.

"We will," said Noah.

"And Mr. Edwin," said Nathan. "You're being good! I really hope you get what you're looking for. I'm sure God's happy that you're doing this His way."

"Yeah," said Noah. "Thanks so much!"

"Tanks so much," repeated Norah.

Edwin smiled. "It's been a long time since someone told me thanks." Then he took a deep breath and pushed the orange raft overboard. It made a huge smacking sound when it flopped onto the water.

Inside the raft, Uncle Jim pulled a handle and turned a

201

small motor on. He began to steer towards land. Ahead of the raft, up the shoreline, Edwin could see the shape of two people. It was a man and a woman. They were jumping and waving. "It must be the kids' parents," Edwin said to himself. He smiled. Then, in the distance, he began to hear the hum of another engine, a big one. No, maybe it was a helicopter.

Uncle Edwin felt the boat slow. His grandson had throttled into a lower speed. He heard Seth talking to his camera on the deck above.

"I heard something," said Seth. "It was a loud splash from behind. I wonder if it was Champ!" The boat was shifted into neutral and Seth climbed back down to the main deck. Edwin found a seat and crossed his legs.

Seth walked towards him, looking confused. "Where, where did everyone go?" he asked.

Grandpa Edwin didn't answer. Instead he started a new conversation.

"Seth, I didn't mean to be selfish," said Edwin. "I'm sorry for griping at you so much."

"Gramps," said Seth. "Where are the kids?" His hand pointed the phone, and the Facetube broadcast, at his Grandpa.

"I guess I'm a little out of check," continued Edwin. "It's tough when your wife and kids are gone. You get left all alone. I guess I'm just a little lost."

"Gramps," continued Seth. "Where'd they go?"

"All I wanted was to give my dad some extra proof for the history books," said Edwin.

"But I heard a splash," said Seth.

Grandpa Edwin looked at Seth. "Oh, that was the kids and their uncle," he said. "Their boat made a loud splash when it hit the water." He pointed towards the boat, now small in size because it had moved so far away.

The sound of the helicopter was steadily growing louder.

"You let them go?!" asked Seth. "What's gotten into you?"

"Well, what's the point of holding them hostage?" asked Edwin. He stood up to confront his grandson. "That's not going to help us get Champ."

"But Gramps, they know who we are!" exclaimed Seth.

Seth turned around, looking towards the sound of the approaching helicopter. He seemed to finally realize what the sound was. He turned back towards Edwin, pointing the pistol at him.

"That sounds like a helicopter!" said Seth. "Is that a helicopter?!"

"Put that thing down dummy," said Grandpa Edwin.

"Did you call the cops?" asked Seth.

"Of course not," said Edwin. "Why would I do a fool thing like that?"

Seth smiled, still pointing the pistol at his grandfather. "Why would you let the Drake family go?" he asked. "My guess is that you're scared. You're scared I'm going to hurt somebody. I am pretty intimidating, right?"

Edwin laughed. "You don't scare me, boy," said Grandpa Edwin. "You don't scare anybody."

Seth cocked the pistol and aimed it at his grandpa.

Edwin stopped laughing. "That's not funny Seth," said Edwin. "What would be the point in shooting me? How will that help you catch Champ?"

"Maybe I don't care anymore," said Seth. "What's the point in catching Champ?"

The helicopter was now overhead. The rhythmic hum from the turning blades was so loud you could feel the vibrations within your belly.

"Forget Champ," said Seth, "I gotta get out of here."

A voice erupted from a loud speaker above. "This is the police Seth Slaughter. Put your gun down and put your hands over your head."

Without thinking, Seth pointed the gun at the chopper and fired all of his bullets towards the cockpit. They ricocheted off the glass, leaving scratches on the window. Seth cackled. He sounded like a mad man. Then, he looked into his phone's camera.

"Do you see that Facetube?" asked Seth. He held the camera up towards the copter. "They think they can get me, but they can't!" He turned the camera back towards his face and continued to laugh. "You know why? Because you'll never catch me coppers!"

Seth ran for the ledge and jumped overboard, into the water. Shots fired from above and Grandpa Edwin fell to the deck. Seth was gone. All that was left was an empty shoe with a smoking hole left near the toe.

CHAPTER 26
FLOAT TRIP

"Police have called an all clear on Lake Champlain," blared a news anchor's voice from Uncle Jim's waterproof radio. "Escaped convict Seth Slaughter is still at large, but officers cite a Facetube video as proof that he's now gone from the area."

A recording from Seth's video was now heard on the radio. "New York, Orlando, St. Louis, who knows where I'm at!" said Seth, laughing. "Actually, I think I'll head towards Mexico, somewhere along the ocean's coast. You know, where I can breathe the salty sea air of the south! Comprende?"

The reporter's voice continued, "Slaughter was last seen on board his yacht at the lake. The yacht appears to be the same one that was recently reported missing by Mean Maud's Boats. Seth was able to escape officers, but not without another bullet wound."

A sound byte from Grandpa Edwin was then played. "That dummy," said Edwin. "He gets shot every time he escapes the police! Now he has a bullet in both feet! Where will he get shot next time, his behind?"

The reporter continued, "Officers captured Edwin Slaughter and are transferring him to a holding cell in Waterbury. Edwin is accused of attempted poaching, two counts of theft and also two counts of kidnapping."

"I didn't mean any harm," said another sound byte from Grandpa Edwin. "I was just being selfish. I'm sorry for causing all this trouble."

Uncle Jim clicked the broadcast off and turned on some music. The sounds of a strumming guitar filled the air. Then Uncle Jim's paddle splashed in the water as he worked to catch up with the rest of the family.

Nathan, Noah, and their mom, Marie, had joined Uncle Jim for a kayak trip on the lake. They had moved up the water while Uncle Jim focused on the news broadcast. Norah and her father were back at camp. They had stayed behind because Norah was taking a nap.

"Mexico?" asked Nathan. "Why would Seth go to Mexico?"

"Duh," said Noah. "To smell the salty sea air of the south! Didn't you hear him?"

Nathan lifted his paddle and splashed a wave of water at

Noah.

"Nathan!" shouted Noah. "I was only kidding."

Marie Drake slapped her paddle on the water, pushing a wave towards Noah. "I'm not!" she said. The three of them splashed back and forth, laughing at each other. Uncle Jim caught up, but he steered clear to avoid the water fight.

"I'm so glad you guys are okay," said Marie. "When I heard those two Slaughters were on the loose again, I flipped my lid! Your dad said I looked so upset, he thought I could breathe fire!"

Uncle Jim slapped his paddle at the water. "See!" he said to the boys. "I told you she breathed fire at your father!"

The boys laughed and Marie looked at Uncle Jim.

"What's this?" she asked with a grin.

"Now, don't breathe fire at me!" said Uncle Jim. "I'm just speaking it like it is!"

"You boys," she said. "Lord knows what you all come up with when you put your heads together."

"I know right?" said Nathan. "But that's how we planned our getaway from the Slaughters!"

"Really?" asked Marie.

"Yeah!" said Noah. "We figured, if we could get the two Slaughters to fight with one another, we could get out of the line of fire and get away."

"And it worked!" said Nathan.

"Oh my goodness," said Marie. "I can't believe you boys. But praise God you're alright!"

"Amen," said Nathan. "And thank God that Champ's alright too!"

"I forgot all about Champ," said Marie. "Did anything

happen?"

"I guess not," said Uncle Jim. "The Slaughters nearly hooked her on a fishing line with their special hook, but then it snapped."

"The line snapped?" asked Marie.

"No!" said Noah. "The hook snapped!"

"Yeah," said Nathan. "Seth went after Champ with his rifle. We heard gun shots, but apparently nothing happened!"

"Is that what the gunshots were?" asked Marie. "That scared me to death. I thought you were in danger."

"We were in danger Mom," said Noah. "But Nathan started preaching at Grandpa Edwin."

Nathan blushed. "Yeah," he said. "I just quoted him scripture. I guess Mr. Edwin let us go because he felt so guilty."

"You two boys are so brave," said Marie. "But what happened to Champ?"

"Got away, I guess," said Noah. "We heard Champ's cry of fury, but then nothing else happened!"

"Yup," said Nathan. "Then Edwin helped us escape. I guess that's when the cops got there."

"Your father and I had been on the phone with them the whole time," said Marie. "They used my phone to find the yacht, and they were just in time. The battery died just when they arrived!"

"Wow," said Noah.

"No kidding," said Nathan.

Everyone was silent for a bit. Nathan thought about the whole event. He could imagine his mom on the phone with the police. She must have been frantic.

The kayaks slipped through the water and Nathan listened to the sound. His paddle splashed as he rowed himself forward. In the distance he heard the splash of a fish jumping from the water. He remembered Champ and a grin appeared on his face.

"Isn't it amazing?" he asked. "I mean, who else gets to see a living dinosaur like Champ?"

"Not many people," said Uncle Jim. "I still remember my first sighting! I was just drifting down the lake one day, just like this! I noticed a huge black snake under the water's surface, only it wasn't a snake. It was Champ's tail! I didn't know any better so I slapped it with my paddle. The rest was history!"

"Yeah," said Noah. "Your boat was history after Champ slapped you back!"

"No kidding," said Marie.

"Oh," said Jim. "It wasn't that bad. It just shook me up a bit."

"And threw you into the air!" said Nathan. "That would be fun!"

"Maybe for you," said Uncle Jim. "But I'll pass on it the next time."

There was another silence as Nathan thought about Uncle Jim's encounter. Maybe he was silly, but he really thought it would have been fun. He could imagine being launched into the air by a backslapping dinosaur. It was almost like flying.

The sound from paddles stirring the water continued as the family moved across the water. Nathan suddenly remembered his conversation with Professor Will at the Creation Museum. He wondered if his mom would be upset about it.

"Mom," said Nathan. "Prof. Will told me that you saw something in the Congo when you were a little girl."

"He did, did he?" asked Marie Drake.

"It was just in passing," said Nathan. "He didn't mean any harm. He thought I already knew."

"Well," said Marie, "something did happen, but I don't talk about it." She took a deep breath. "Your father's such a skeptic, I just keep my mouth closed."

"So it's true?" asked Nathan.

Marie smiled at him. "Yes, it's true," she said.

"Was it Mokele-mbembe?" asked Noah. "Dr. Great was talking about a dinosaur named Mokele-mbembe when I was on my dinosaur dig!"

"Not the dig again," said Nathan. "You're always talking about the dig."

"Oh Nathan, leave it alone," said Noah.

Marie Drake splashed them both with her paddle. The boys looked at her in surprise.

"Yes," said Marie. "I saw Mokele-mbembe."

"Cool!" said Uncle Jim.

"Well, no. It really wasn't that cool," said Marie. "Mokele-mbembe wasn't a nice dinosaur. He was scary, and I hope I never have to see him again."

"Really?" asked Nathan.

"Yes," said Marie. "He's as big as an elephant, and his temper is even bigger. He's powerful too. He's able to stop the flow of the rivers. Well, at least that's what his name,

Mokele-mbembe, means in the local language."

"Whoa," said Noah.

"Wow," said Nathan. "Thank goodness Champ is so nice."

"Well," said Uncle Jim. "Champ's only nice if you're nice. If you don't bother her, she won't bother you."

Nathan thought about Uncle Jim hitting Champ with the paddle again. He supposed that wasn't very nice. But it still sounded fun.

"Speaking of Champ," said Noah, "look up ahead. There's an awful lot of bubbles floating up from under the water."

"Cool!" said Nathan. "We're heading right into them!"

"Uh, this isn't good," said Marie. "Jim, what's happening?"

"All right," said Uncle Jim. "It's all right, nobody panic."

"I'm not panicking," said Noah.

"Yeah, who's panicking?" said Nathan.

"Boys, be quiet." said Marie. "This is serious."

The kayaks continued floating forward. The Drakes could no longer steer around the bubbles because they were too close. It was too late to steer around. Nathan looked at Noah and grinned. He was excited that they were getting to see Champ.

"What do we do?" asked Marie.

"Here's the plan," said Uncle Jim. "Everyone pick up your paddle and put it on your lap."

Everyone did as Uncle Jim suggested.

Marie spoke to herself. "Thank God Norah's back at camp with her father," she said.

"Now, keep your hands to yourself," said Uncle Jim. "Don't touch the water. Just look into it. You're about to get an awesome view of a living dinosaur!"

"Shoot," said Noah. "I wish I had my camera!"

"I see her," said Marie. "I see her!"

Nathan saw Champ too. Below the surface, her long black tail was swishing back and forth. Flippers could be seen a little deeper. It looked like Champ was doing a gentle belly roll in the water, like she was playing.

"This is so cool!" said Noah.

"She's beautiful," said Marie. "Like a giant water giraffe, just minding her own business."

"That tail looks awfully strong," said Nathan. "What do you think will happen if I hit her with my paddle?"

"We know what will happen Nathan," said Noah. "She'll hit you back! She might hit us too!"

Nathan grinned.

"Don't tease Nathan," said Marie.

"Who's teasing?" he asked. He lifted his paddle into the air, ready to strike. "It sounds so fun! She won't hurt us."

"Nathan!" screamed Marie. But she was too late. Nathan brought his paddle down hard onto the dinosaur's tail.

212

CHAPTER 27
JAIL TIME

The doors to Edwin's jail cell slid shut with a clang.

"I finally made it to the slammer," he said to himself. "I guess I'm getting what I deserve."

He looked around the room and took a quick inventory. Three solid block walls surrounded him, the fourth wall was a series of iron bars, and a toilet sat next to a sink in a back corner. On the opposite corner was a bunk bed. The top bunk was empty, but the bottom was full. A sheet, covering a large man, moved up and down as a man slept. He rolled to one side and flopped out a large, muscular arm.

"You are a mountain of a man," Edwin said out loud. "I

hope you're nice."

The man snored.

Edwin made his way to the bed. The day had been long and tiring and he was worn out. He had come so close to getting his life long desire, catching the old dragon named Champ. He even had the beast hooked on the line, but somehow the hook broke! How could that happen? His dad had used the hook for years without a problem. That was a long time ago, was it possible that the hook was too old to work? Was metal capable of growing old and tired?

Looking back now, Edwin wondered if he had gone into shock from losing Champ. The capture and loss had made Edwin speechless. He had lost his breath and his body felt like it would crumple to the ground. It took all his strength to keep standing.

During the spell, Edwin's eyesight flashed white and it was hard to see. At one point he heard the young Drake kid speaking to him. Nathan had accused him of not being a Christian. That's what woke Edwin up, both physically and spiritually.

The young boy challenged Edwin to prove his love for God. Nobody had ever done that before. Nathan had said Edwin couldn't be a Christian because of the way he acted. Was the boy right? Did Edwin not love the Lord?

The question seemed foreign. It had been a long time since Edwin asked himself questions like that. Am I a Christian? Can people tell that I'm a Christian? Do I show it by the way I act? Am I good? Would my example give them a desire to follow God?

Edwin shook his head. He had tried to be a good man his

whole life, but somehow he'd taken a wrong turn. "How did I get to this place?" he asked out loud.

"Lord, I've done a lot of bad things," said Edwin. "Is that why I'm here? I've been selfish and I've ignored how it hurt others. I've especially hurt my family and those Drake kids. They must have been scared to death, talking to me like that on the yacht. That took guts!"

Edwin climbed to the top bunk of the bed. It would be nice to lie down. Unfortunately the mattress didn't offer much comfort. It was stiff as a board.

Edwin noticed writing on the ceiling above him. There were messages from more than one prisoner. The first one read, "Joey was here." The second said "Don't mess with the gold-toothed guard." The last one said "I'm going to die here alone." A chill ran up Edwin's spine. Dying alone in a prison was a terrible thought.

Edwin suddenly felt guilty. The weight of wrong decisions fell on him and it was too much to bear. His eyes filled with tears and Edwin sobbed. He felt lonesome, alone in a prison, with a trail of selfishness behind him. He'd hurt Seth. He'd hurt Nathan, Noah, Norah and their family. He'd even hurt Frankie. Poor Frankie was hurt the most. All the big oaf ever wanted was for somebody to care, and Edwin left him like he was yesterday's dirty laundry.

Edwin remembered their last meeting. He had hoped to break Frankie out of jail, just like he'd helped Seth get out. Frankie refused. He had changed sides and turned good. He was even going to turn Edwin in to the prison guard.

"God bless Frankie," Edwin said to himself. "He was just trying to be a good boy."

215

Edwin looked at the writing on the ceiling. "I'm going to die here alone," he read out loud. "I hope not. At least, not like this."

Edwin sat up and leaned against the cold block wall of the prison cell. He looked at the prison bars and took a deep breath. "Now I see why Frankie couldn't stand staying in jail, even if it was only three whole days. Well I guess it's been a lot more now, poor kid."

Edwin noticed the man on the bunk below was no longer snoring. He figured he'd better wrap up his little conversation with God. It wasn't much of a conversation yet, but that's because Edwin was stalling.

"Lord," said Edwin, "I'm sorry. I've been bad and I'm sorry for what I've done. Could you ever forgive me? Could you forgive me for what I've done? I let a criminal loose and I lit a fire under him. I kidnapped some kids and I tried to steal what wasn't mine. Can you forgive me?"

The silence of the prison cell answered Edwin's request. He felt even more alone and let out another sob.

"God," he moaned. "Can you forgive me for what I've done to Frankie?"

The man below stirred. Edwin tried to pull himself together.

"What?"mumbled the man. "Wha, what? What was that?"

"Uh," said Edwin. "I'm sorry big guy. I was just talking to God. I'm sorry for waking you up."

"What?" said the voice below. "Gramps? Gramps, is that you?" The man stood up beside the bed, and Edwin saw his grandson Frankie.

"Frankie?" asked Edwin. "Frankie, is it really you?"

"What are you doing here Gramps?" asked Frankie.

Edwin dropped from the bed and looked at his grandson. He hesitated for a moment, then jumped forward and grabbed Frankie in a hug. Frankie hugged back.

"What's going on?" asked Frankie. "Why are you here?"

"Oh, it's a long story Frankie," said Edwin. "And I bet I've got plenty of time to tell it! But can it wait till tomorrow? I'm worn out."

Frankie smiled a goofy grin. "Of course Gramps. Whatever you say."

Edwin grabbed Frankie's arm and looked into his eyes.

"Frankie," he said. "Can you forgive me for what I've done to you? Can you forgive me for leaving you all alone?"

Frankie smiled. "I already have grandpa," he said. "You're already forgiven."

CHAPTER 28
MEAN MAUD

"I need one more signature at the bottom of the page, right here," said the police officer.

Maud signed her name and put the pen down. "Is that it?"

"Yes ma'am," said the man. "The boat is yours again. Although, it is funny how Seth Slaughter asked somebody named Maud for a boat."

Maud looked at the officer. "What's that supposed to mean?" she asked.

"Well," said the officer, "seeing how your boat was the one given to him."

"I don't know what you're talking about," said Maud. "That boat was stolen, probably by Seth Slaughter himself. Why would I report a missing boat if I had given it to him?"

"I don't know," said the officer. "That's the part that doesn't make sense. But it is awfully interesting. At least, you have to admit it's an interesting coincidence."

"You're right," said Maud. "It is a coincidence." She pushed an intercom button on her desk and spoke to her secretary. "Laura, our work in here is done. Could you please show this nice officer to the door?"

"Yes ma'am, right away," said a secretary's voice from the other end of the intercom.

Maud looked at the officer and politely smiled. "Thank you so much for your time, and for returning our yacht," she said.

The door to the office opened from the outside and Laura stood waiting.

The officer nodded, walked towards the door and turned around. "You're welcome Mrs. Maud, and thank you for your time." He turned to Laura and said, "It's okay. I know the way out."

Laura nodded and watched the officer leave. Then she turned towards Maud and said, "He's gone ma'am."

Maud leaned her head back and let out a sigh of relief.

"That was close," she said. "Though I have been in tighter spots."

"Did he suspect something?" asked Laura.

"Oh, he suspected something alright," said Maud. "But he didn't have any proof."

"Let's hope he doesn't find it," said Laura.

"He won't find any," said Maud. "I can cover my tracks."

"Most of them," said Laura. "I've got bad news." She threw a newspaper on Maud's desk. The headline read 'Second Artifact Stolen From Useless, Old Museum'.

"What do they mean useless, old museum?" asked Maud. "How rude, that's my dad's stuff they're talking about. It's not useless."

"I thought it was rude too," said Laura. "The story wasn't bad though. They don't say much about your dad, but they do talk about the museum. Maybe the free advertising will bring in some more business."

Maud looked up at Laura. "You always look at the bright side of things, don't you Laura?"

"I try," said Laura. She sat down in a chair that faced Maud. "I have a bit of good news for you too. I finally heard from the gun restorer."

Maud looked up from the newspaper. "Is it done yet?" she asked.

"Yes ma'am," said Laura. "They said the Dragon Killer could have been a complete loss, but they were able to save it. It's now firing like a Gatling gun should."

"Excellent!" said Maud. "That's the best news I've had all week!"

"Would you like me to have it put back in the museum?" asked Laura.

"Of course not," said Maud. "I can't risk it being stolen again. That's why I replaced all of Dad's stuff with fakes. That's also why we put bars on the windows."

"Yes ma'am," said Laura.

"But somehow," continued Maud, "that goofball brother

of mine still got in the museum. He's smarter than he looks! He stole Dad's hook, or at least the fake copy of it, he messed up Penny the gorilla and he ruined a perfectly good air-conditioner in the staff lunch room."

"By the way," said Laura. "I spoke to our taxidermist yesterday. Penny will be back on display next week. Or do you want us to create a copy of her too?"

Maud smiled at her secretary. "No, we don't need a copy of Penny. I don't think my brother will bother her again. I have an idea that will stop him in his tracks."

"Jail, ma'am?" asked Laura.

"Oh no, no," said Maud. "We'll get him out of that. My brother's not a criminal, he's just old, tired and out of money. I think he feels stuck, like he's in a corner with no more options. You'd be surprised what a person can do when they're like that."

"Then what ma'am?" asked Laura.

"A little charity," said Maud. "We're going to give him what he wants."

Laura raised an eyebrow in suspicion. "Champ, ma'am?"

"That's right," said Maud. "We're going to give him Champ."

Laura leaned forward. "With all due respect ma'am, this doesn't sound like you. What are you really planning?"

"Oh, I promise Laura. There are no strings attached on this one," said Maud. "I'm really going to help Edwin. You see, I'm tired of my family looking like a bunch of fools. This whole dragon business, chasing after Champ, has taken its toll on the Slaughters." Maud slammed her fist down on her desk. "They called Dad a stubborn, old fool! A fool, Laura!

He wasn't a fool."

"No ma'am," said Laura.

"He really did catch Champ," said Maud. "But Champ was taken away, everything Dad had was taken away."

A tear slowly dripped down Maud's face. "It's horrible, watching your father shrivel up like a piece of old fruit. He couldn't find a reason to live after they took Champ. He withered up and died."

Laura handed a tissue to Maud.

"Thank you," said Maud. She dabbed the tears from her face and took a deep breath.

"I don't want the same thing to happen to my brother Edwin," said Maud. "He's had everything taken from him too. I know I've kept my distance from him, we have our differences, but he is my brother."

"That's correct, ma'am," said Laura.

"I don't want him to wither and die like Dad," said Maud.

"I understand ma'am," said Laura. "That's very big of you ma'am."

"Well, no," said Maud. "He's family, and we take care of our family." She dabbed her face with the tissue again. "Besides, if we set this up right, we can use it to make a lot of money!"

"I knew there was a catch," said Laura.

"It's a win-win situation," said Maud. "Edwin gets what he wants, and we benefit from giving it to him!"

223

Author Bio

Ben Russell is that dinosaur guy. Yes, there's a fossil skeleton overlooking the bed in his bedroom. Imagine what his wife thinks. He loves Biblical creation and his inner child gets excited about dinosaurs and the idea that they're not millions of years old. Evolution? Ben says that's just a theory that turns people from God.

Ben is a family man. He and his lovely wife have four happy kids, a clowder of cats, a brood of chickens and a hungry herd of goats. They make their home among the roaming hills of the Missouri Ozarks. The Russells, not the animals. Well, they all live there together, but the animals live outside. Ben writes Juvenile/Middle Grade Fiction Adventures when he's not chasing after chickens or building fences for his goats.

Author Notes

I realized I had a problem when I set out to write the second book in the Noah Drake Dragon series. I had a list of characters from the first book that I wanted to carry over, but I didn't feel like I knew many of them. Who were they? What made them tick?

Two characters seem to stand out from the others in book one, Nathan Drake and Frankie Slaughter. I think they both stood out because I knew what made them both tick. I knew their personalities. Unfortunately, Frankie would be limited in book 2 because he was in jail. So I created Frankie's brother Seth. I knew Frankie had family, I just didn't know who they were yet. Other family members could come into play later in the series, but right now I only have plans for Maud. We'll talk about her in a bit.

In my mind, Seth Slaughter was the anti-Frankie. He has a lot of the same personalities, but he's mean just for the sake of being mean. He's not the polar opposite of Frankie though. In fact, he's a lot like Frankie, except he's mean. When I created Seth, I wanted him to have something to distinguish who he was. Some dependency that would agitate him if he didn't have it. At first, it was simple, it was going to be a lollipop. He would always need a lollipop in his mouth to be happy, that was his stress reliever. In fact, there is one place in the book where I wrote in a lollipop. But I decided to take his dependency to the next level. We needed something that would break the monotony, something that could be entertaining. So a star was born! Perhaps I should say a Facetube star was born. Seth needed a phone, and not just any phone! He needed one that would record or broadcast to Faectube! If he can't have that, look out!

My next challenging character was Noah Drake. I knew who I wanted Noah to be, but I don't think I wrote him out enough in book one. The series is named after Noah Drake, so I better make him more of a character. I tried in book 1, but his brother stole the spotlight, Nathan is more entertaining. But Noah is the mystery solver. He's not really a brainiac, but he is smarter than the average person and he's the one that can always figure things out. He can solve any puzzle and he's the one that always gets the family out of trouble. I hope, after reading book 2, you know and like Noah a little more.

Book 2 also introduced another member of the Slaughter family, Mean Maud. Maud is an interesting character and she will definitely come into play in book 3. I tried to keep her a secret for as long as possible. In the end, I laid it all out on the table, but she's still a bit of a mystery. I can tell you that she's been behind the scenes the whole time. Maud is more of the brains in her family. She's not brilliant, like Noah, but she is a no-nonsense person who set out to find success. Maud has a heart, especially for her family, but usually she can figure out a way to make a dollar out of it. That's what she'll do with her family's problems in book 3! Will the Drake family interfere once again? Well, we'll have to see.

One of my goals in the Noah Drake series is to share my love for Biblical creation. When I finished Book 2, I was worried that I didn't have as much cool creation information as book one. In hindsight though, it seems I overcompensated and put in more! I hope it's not too much! I'm excited if you can learn, but I want you to enjoy the book and have fun too.

I really enjoy writing the Noah Drake series, but I have to admit I'm really not a writer. At least, I never thought I was. Instead, I'm an audio-video guy. I went to college and studied radio broadcast and film. I then went on to work in radio, television, and media. I enjoy putting together a good production for broadcast, but I no longer do it professionally. It didn't provide for the family the way I wanted. Oh, I still dabble in it. Currently I produce a professional live broadcast for our church's Sunday services. Noah Drake was a way for me to step out on my own and start an independent business. It's a lot of work! Being an author is not just about writing, it's also about marketing, advertising, and all the things in between. I've learned a lot and I still continue to learn!

I hope you have enjoyed the Noah Drake series! If you did, I would really appreciate your review on Amazon. Your review really helps! Books with reviews, even negative ones, tend to sell better. Your review helps others decide whether or not it's worth their money. Honestly I can't write a whole lot, or support my family, without selling books. It would be a TREMENDOUS blessing if you could take two minutes to go on Amazon and quickly say what you thought of Noah Drake and why. Just go to https://www.amazon.com/review/create-review?asin=198129080X. Thanks so much!

If you're interested in learning more about Biblical creation, download my free book! Several creation teachers, speakers and authors have let me use portions of their books to share in my own Biblical creation compilation! You'll learn biology from Kent Hovind, astronomy from Dr. Edward Boudreaux, archaeology with Dr. Dennis Swift, and dragon legends from Dennis Petersen. This book is not a simple read, but it has some excellent information if you're interested in more about Biblical creation. Plus it will point you towards excellent authorities who can help you dig deeper!

I'm also toying around with the idea of writing a short story about Uncle Jim. It would be a pre story to book one. It's not yet done, however I have started it. I'll give you a heads up when it's complete. I'll probably send it to you for free if you're on my email list. You can join my list, and get the free biblical creation book at http://creationtales.com/free .

Thanks again for reading, and I pray God richly blesses you!

Curious About Creation?

I am, and you'll love this book if you are too! You can get CREATION FOR NEWBIES for FREE when you sign up for my newsletter! This exclusive book includes in depth information from the leading biblical creation teachers and scientists!

You'll learn biology from Kent Hovind, astronomy from Dr. Edward Boudreaux, archaeology with Dr. Dennis Swift, and dragon legends with Dennis Petersen.

Get your free copy now and start learning more about how creation could be real! Plus my newsletter will give you surprise freebies and updates about upcoming book releases!

Download your copy at http://creationtales.com/free

Made in the USA
Monee, IL
17 July 2020